Cl

CHERRY

CANYON

Also by Mike Attebery

On/Off

Billionaires, Bullets, Exploding Monkeys

Seattle On Ice

Bloody Pulp

Rosé in Saint Tropez

CHOKE CHERRY CANYON

by
Mike Attebery

Cryptic Bindings

Seattle

Chokecherry Canyon

www.mikeattebery.com

First Edition: August 2017

ISBN: 978-0-692-88826-1

Publisher's Note:
This is a work of fiction. Names, characters, places, and incidents
are either the product of the author's imagination or are used
fictitiously, any resemblance to actual persons (living or dead),
business establishments, events, or locales is coincidental.

Printed in the United States of America.

For Shirley

Farmington, New Mexico

A coyote scampered across the street and disappeared into the bushes as the car's headlights swept across the dirt parking lot. The vehicle pulled up to the front of the crumbling stucco building, exhaust fumes visible in the wintery desert air. The driver killed the lights, climbed out, and headed up the walk to the entrance, where a red neon sign in the front window flashed "*Caliente! – Mexican Eatery.*" With each flash, the garish sign fleetingly illuminated the abandoned downtown streets that surrounded the low-rent eatery.

Inside, the place was all but deserted. Pendant lights hung over scattered tables and booths, casting them in pools of dim light that took on a feverish glow whenever the sign's crimson light pulsed across the room. A waitress met the man at the door, carefully avoiding eye contact as she led him across the room to a table in the far back corner, where an overweight, balding diner in his mid-fifties sat in the shadows, his broad shoulders hunched over a plate of seared meat strips and vegetables. His coat was tossed on the seat beside him. The strobing light gave his polyester shirt a translucent quality, continually revealing the outline of his undershirt beneath. He grabbed a steamed tortilla in one beefy hand, piled it high with meat, peppers, and guacamole, and took a massive bite.

The waitress left without offering the newcomer a drink or bringing him a menu; his demeanor told her he wouldn't be staying long.

The new arrival, a man in his early forties, with a thick moustache and flat, black eyes, took off his wide-brimmed hat and sat down. He scanned the table, his eyes lingering on the jagged edge of a serrated steak knife that sat just to the side of the dining man's plate. The teeth glittered as the neon sign flashed on and off.

"How you been, Harvey?" the man asked as his eyes traveled from the knife blade to the sweating man across the table.

The bald man looked up, wiping guacamole from his mouth with his shirtsleeve. "Fine 'til you got here." He snatched up the knife and sliced off another chunk of meat, which he pulled from the blade with his teeth. "How did I know they'd be sending *you?*"

The man watched with disgust as Harvey assembled another messy fajita. The meat's fatty red juices glistened on the plate as he returned the knife to the table. Just as Harvey was about to take another bite, the man set a thick envelope on the table between them.

Harvey lowered his hands and studied the envelope warily. "What the hell is that?"

"Open it."

Harvey bit off another mouthful, set the remainder on his plate, and slid it away. The plate clinked against the edge of the knife as Harvey pulled the envelope open and ran his chubby fingers through two thick wads of crisp, clean hundred dollar bills. He thumbed through one of the bundles and looked up.

"It's a start. I assume there'll be more where this came from."

The man shook his head. "One and done, Harvey."

"They think *this* will keep me quiet?" Harvey sputtered. "They owe me a whole hell of a lot more than a *one-time* payment. This is just an insult-"

"*They* don't owe you jack-shit. You should be grateful they're offering you this much. I suggest you take it and keep your fat mouth shut. Or better yet, pocket the money and get the hell out of town."

Harvey slashed off another piece of meat and shoved it in his mouth. The blade flared in the light as his hand quivered angrily.

"So now you think I should leave town. Listen, *son*, don't go giving me advice, okay, because I could squash you."

"Those days are long gone," the man said as his eyes again locked on the glint of the blade.

"Don't forget, I know *everything* that's going on here. The folks you're working for know exactly what it will take to keep me quiet." His cheeks flushed with anger as his eyes narrowed. "So go back and tell them that unless they want me to take this public, they're gonna have to meet with me *in person* and work out another long-term arrangement." He slammed down the knife and shoved the envelope back across the table. "And you can tell them to keep the chump change. I want a piece of the pie, not some bullshit bribe."

The man across the table sat quietly, the muscles in his jaw tensing and relaxing as he seemed to consider the demand. Beneath the table, he was quietly pulling leather gloves onto his calloused hands.

Harvey used the lull in conversation to fix himself another messy portion. "Don't think for a minute that I won't talk," he mumbled as he again shoveled food into his mouth.

"Oh, I don't doubt you, Harvey," The man said as he calmly slid the envelope into his coat pocket, stood, and pulled on his hat. "The problem is, I was sent here with two options, and accepting a counter-offer wasn't one of them."

Harvey glanced up at him from the corner of his eye.

Suddenly, the man grabbed the steak knife in his gloved hand and brought it to Harvey's throat. The edge of the serrated blade bit into the bulge of Harvey's sweaty neck. Harvey's eyes bulged in abject horror as air wheezed from his stunned mouth. Then the blade sank into the flesh of his throat, cutting a path deep into his windpipe. Hot air and burbling blood coursed through the attacker's gloved fingers as he held the blade tight and sawed deeper and deeper into Harvey's neck. His other hand was clasped over Harvey's mouth, pushing his head against the back of the booth. The man stayed that way, stealing a glance over his shoulder at the empty restaurant. Even through the leather, he could feel hot, wet air seeping from Harvey's mouth. After a moment, he released his grip, dropped the knife onto the seat he'd so recently vacated, and let go of the heavy-set man's body. Harvey slumped forward, his head bouncing on the table with a sickening thud.

Harvey's killer pulled the gloves from his hands and slipped them into his pockets, then he turned and walked out of the restaurant, snatching a peppermint from a dish by the register as he headed out the door.

Harvey's head lay resting on the table. His lifeless eyes stared straight ahead as the red light flashed on and off. On and off. The blood continued to course from the gaping wound in his neck, soaking into the tablecloth and saturating the fabric.

Mike Attebery

1.

Red and blue lights whirled around the dusty lot as uniformed police officers headed in and out of the building. The neon *Caliente!* sign had been switched off in an effort to avoid drawing attention to the crime scene, but the lights from the squad cars more than made up the difference.

Two guys in dark blue, zip-up jumpsuits pulled a gurney from the coroner's van and were just wheeling it up the front walk as a weathered '68 Mustang convertible pulled into the lot and parked in the far corner. The car's paint was ostensibly black, but like its owner, dust and grime, and years of indifference had left it weathered and streaked with gray.

Luke Murphy, boyishly handsome, with uncombed salt and pepper hair, picked through the layers of newspapers and magazines littering the passenger seat 'til he located a reporter's notebook. He climbed out of the car, feeling significantly older than his 33 years, and forced the driver's side door closed behind him. The door resisted, groaning irritably, before its hinges popped and the door slammed shut with a metallic clang.

Luke took in the scene. It wasn't every day Farmington saw this kind of action. At least, not this *particular* part of Farmington. Judging from the pace at which the jumpsuit guys were walking, and the gurney and zippered bag they were bringing along with them, someone had just eaten their last meal in this dive.

Homicides, rare as they might be, were much more common around the bars on Main Street or in some of the more questionable establishments near the river. This place, while it would never be listed in a Zagat guide, was in a relatively benign neighborhood. It was the kind of place where working class families took their kids for a rare dinner out.

Luke flipped to a blank page in his notebook and dug through his coat pockets in search of a pen. He located a crinkling bag of corn nuts before he found a BIC, and popped a few toasted kernels in his mouth as he made his way into the restaurant.

The place was hot and crowded and thick with the pungent odor of copper and raw hamburger meat. Luke's nose crinkled. He'd reported from one or two similar crime scenes over the years, and each time, those elemental smells had accompanied memorably gory displays.

Camera flashes were coming from an area near the back, and Luke picked up his pace, making a reluctant beeline for the hub of activity. He spotted a man in a brown suit and tie, talking to a uniformed officer by the entrance to the kitchen. A serious expression was etched on his face. He was surprisingly young for someone in a supervisory position, exactly Luke's age in fact.

Luke knew Sonny West fairly well. They'd gone to high school together. And though they'd never been *friends* in that long-ago life, they had, over time, developed that familiarity common amongst townies and those who have boomeranged home in the decade or so since graduation. That, and the fact that Luke was the youngest reporter at *The Farmington Daily Times,* ensured that he and his former classmate crossed paths at least once or twice a week, usually at the scenes of car accidents and store robberies.

Sonny was motioning with his hands as he spoke, and in so doing, turned to see Luke heading his way. Sonny waved him over, interrupting the conversation with his uniformed associate as Luke approached.

"Murphy, how you doing? I had a feeling you'd be the guy covering this tonight."

"Usually a safe bet. It comes with being on the losing side of seniority," Luke replied as he shook Sonny's hand. "What happened here?"

"Best we can tell, couple guys got into an

argument over dinner and things got... stabby. Fella at the table there was damn near decapitated. Table looks like it was dunked in Heinz 57."

"Shit."

"Fuckin' mess." Sonny said as he wiped his boots on the restaurant's carpeting. "I've got blood all over my soles."

Luke's lip curled. "Who should I be talking to?"

Sonny looked up from his boots and motioned to a guy standing near the front counter. He looked to be around Luke's age, maybe a year or two older, with a full beard and a much more casual outfit than what Sonny sported on the job.

"New guy's handling this one," Sonny mused. "Hot shot detective, just moved here from Seattle."

"Who is he?" Luke asked.

"Detective Gridley. *Mick* Gridley. That an absurd name or what?"

No more than 'Sonny,' Luke thought.

Instead, he just nodded his head, making an effort to keep the peace without agreeing with what struck him as a pissy, smalltown comment. Locals, especially folks like Sonny West, who had quite possibly never left the Four Corners region, were never too happy when people with names like "Mick" got prime gigs around town. Hell, the fact that Luke himself had left the area for the better part of a decade, before skulking back last year to

16

take care of his now deceased father, had earned him a reputation as an outsider in his own right, even though he had gone to high school with 90 percent of the Farmington Police Department's boys in blue. For the most part, Sonny treated him like he always had, but depending on the officer, and depending on the incident he was covering, more often than not, Luke still found himself on the outs with law enforcement.

"Come on," Sonny said. "I'll introduce you."

Detective Gridley was questioning a waitress who stood at the front register, refilling a bowl of mints. Judging by the look on the detective's face, and the intensity with which the waitress was attending to the candy dish, Luke guessed very little information was being transferred.

Gridley saw Sonny and Luke heading his way and wrapped up the line of questioning. "Okay, I think that's all for now," he muttered as he took out a small spiral-bound notebook similar to the one Luke was holding. "I just need your phone number in case I have to get in touch with you."

The waitress rattled off her contact information, then headed into the kitchen.

"By the way," Sonny told Luke as they crossed the restaurant, "they're gonna be hauling the body out of there in a few minutes – soon as we can get some more muscle in here to help – he's a *big guy*. But if you want some pictures, don't wait too long."

Luke nodded. "Will do."

For a small town paper, *The Times'* readers were remarkably fond of Weegee-style snuff shots.

"And *this,*" Sonny continued, "Is Detective Mick Gridley. Detective, this is Luke Murphy, reporter for *The Daily Times.*"

Gridley passed the notebook to his left hand and reached out with his right. "Pleased to meet you, Murphy," he said as he shook Luke's hand.

"You too. So what happened here? Who is this guy?" He saw Gridley draw up his reporter's pad. "Nice notebook by the way-"

Gridley glanced at the matching journal in Luke's hand, gave a half-hearted smile, and jumped in, leading the way to the body as he relayed the facts of the case.

"From what we can piece together, the victim is Harvey Pouch. In his mid-50s. Owned a pool and spa company on the edge of town. Came in a few nights a week to eat dinner and drink himself into a stupor. Been coming here for years."

Luke jotted down the name.

"Anyone see who did it? Any sort of description?"

"Man came in around ten o'clock. Waitress says she didn't get a good look at him. She *claims* she heard no disturbance, no shouting or arguing. Guy left, and she just figured Pouch had passed out at his table like usual. She didn't know anything had happened till she went back with his customary third margarita, and found him face down in a puddle of his own blood."

"And the weapon?" Luke asked.

"Steak knife. Slashed his throat."

Luke grimaced, unconsciously bringing one hand up to his neck.

"Yeah," Gridley empathized. "Pretty nasty. Cheap serrated number, too. Must've hurt like hell. Detective friend of mine up in Seattle saw something similar not too long ago. Even happened in a Mexican restaurant of all places. Poor son of a bitch just wanted a fajita. Ended up drowning in a pool of B positive. The irony."

One of the uniformed officers approached Gridley.

"If you're all finished here, we're ready to take the body."

Gridley turned to Luke. "You need those pictures?"

"Yeah," Luke replied reluctantly. "I suppose I do."

He headed through the crowd of officers, pulling a digital camera from his pocket as he stepped up onto the bench of a neighboring table and held the camera over his head, quickly framing the body in the middle of the screen, and firing off one shot and a safety. He checked the photos and glanced over at the seat opposite the body. His eyes fell on the bloody steak knife lying on the bench. He looked over at Gridley and nodded that he was done.

"All right, fellas," Gridley said. "He's all yours."

The officers moved out of the way. One of them bumped into Luke as he stepped down from the table, and stopped to give him a withering, silent stare. Luke stepped aside, inadvertently making eye contact with Gridley, who happened to catch the interaction and arched his eyebrows as the officer walked away.

Then the guys in the jumpsuits rolled the late Harvey Pouch out of his booth and onto the floor, where they zipped him into a white body bag, heaved him up onto the gurney, and rolled him out past the salad bar.

~

The last remaining police cars were pulling out of the parking lot as Luke and Gridley left the restaurant. Now that the initial excitement of a bloody crime scene had been taken in, and the body was en route to the medical examiner's office, the restaurant would be turned over to the crime scene unit to document every inch of the place. In a few days, the restaurant owners would be given the go-ahead to scrub down the tables and once more serve enchiladas where Harvey Pouch had sliced his last fajita.

Luke made a mental note to steer clear of Harvey's booth if he ever came here for dinner..

They stopped in the middle of the dirt lot.

"Was that knife in there the murder weapon?"

"Looks that way," Gridley replied. "Whoever did it sure wasn't worried about leaving evidence behind. It also looks like he was wearing gloves, which in my mind makes this whole thing premeditated."

Luke looked over his notes. "I think that's everything for now." He pulled a business card out of his back pocket and handed it to Gridley. "If you get any more information, I'd appreciate a call."

Gridley looked at the number on the card. For a moment it looked as though he wanted to ask a question, but then he just nodded his head, reached out, and again shook Luke's hand.

"I'll be in touch," he said.

2.

Even for Farmington, *The Daily Times* offices were a sleepy place most weekday mornings. The majority of the staff, many of whom had been with the paper for decades, tended to roll in around 9 or 10 a.m., *long* after the latest edition had hit driveways and been consumed at kitchen tables and diners around town. Most of the news writers felt that they had long ago put in their time on the front lines – so the very idea of getting to their desks at 8 a.m. or *anytime* before then, was utterly incomprehensible to them. That left the early shift to the guy with the least seniority: Luke Murphy. Since that same junior standing was the reason he'd been at the previous night's crime scene until well past midnight, Luke was very much the worse for wear as he dumped a packet of creamer into his mug of coffee and looked over the article he'd thrown together moments before that morning's edition had gone to press. The headline on the front page read *MAN KILLED IN MEXICAN RESTAURANT.* As Luke reread the article, cringing at a couple of typos that had escaped his fuzzy eyes, Red Sanders, the *Times'* 65 year-old Editor-in-Chief, walked up behind him. Red adjusted his signature thick, black glasses, which popped out against the background of his short, white hair, and patted Luke on the shoulder.

"Great work last night," Red said. " And just a couple of typos this time."

"*Gruesome* work, and thanks for noticing. I could barely keep my eyes straight while I was proofing it."

Red laughed. "Don't sweat it. We've all been there. It's a good piece either way. You get any sleep?"

"Not a wink."

"I remember those days. The late shift's a lot of fun, isn't it?"

"If you say so, Red." Luke wiped his eyes and took a sip of coffee. "I just want to get home and pass out."

"Not so fast. You didn't forget about the ceremony for Ben Gerritt today, did you?"

"Ben Gerritt? Oh damn. Yeah, it completely slipped my mind. We're definitely covering it?"

"You bet your ass we're covering it! Aside from that restaurant murder, this is the biggest news in town. What's more, the guy *owns* this paper! We don't cover it and we're all out of work." He glanced at his watch. "I should be heading over there now. Why don't I bum a ride with you?"

Luke paused a beat, taking a deep breath and

forcing himself to get going. Then he jumped to his feet, grabbing his windbreaker as he started across the room. If he didn't get moving and *stay* moving, he'd be dead on his feet before he made it to the parking lot. "I guess it's now or never."

Red followed close behind. "That's my boy."

They headed for the front door, passing an old man in a purple baseball cap and overalls, who looked to be in at *least* his early 80s. He was banging his hands on the front counter as Grace, the paper's receptionist, tried to calm him.

"My wife can't get any sleep!" he cried. "We've called the police, but they won't do anything. These trucks just keep coming past our house every night. All night long."

"Sir, I'm not sure how we can help you," Grace replied.

"The city doesn't seem to give a damn. Can't you guys send someone out to see it for themselves? Give it some coverage? I'm telling you, these trucks are enormous, a dozen of them at least. They drive into the canyon around midnight every night, and they just keep coming..."

The man's complaints faded into the background as Luke and Red headed out the door. Luke led the way to his beat-up Mustang. The top was still down.

"Don't you ever lock your car, son?" Red asked.

Luke waved him off. "There's nothing in this car

worth stealing, let alone the car itself."

Red nodded, making no argument as he opened the creaking passenger door.

"I'm warning you now," Luke said. "You're in the hands of a man who's been awake for just about twenty six hours."

"I'm sure you're as fit as a fiddle."

"I'll be honest with you, Red," Luke said as he opened his door and got in. "The fact that you put it that way makes me question your judgment."

~

The location of the press event was still very much a construction scene. Several half-completed buildings and cranes towered above the crowd of dignitaries, news reporters, and assorted Farmington residents who had turned up for the event. A banner suspended from one of the buildings read *"Gerritt Arena: Making Farmington Great Again!"* Several signs for Dupuis Construction were secured to the chain link fencing that surrounded the majority of the structures.

Luke took in the scene, noting a broadcast truck for KOB Eyewitness News that was parked in the back of the crowd. A camera crew was shooting from the top of one of Dupuis Construction's field-office trailers. A speaking area had been erected between the half-completed arena and a towering support building to the west. That building had been the first structure topped off in the massive complex. So far, *no one* had gotten a look inside, but as far as Luke could gather, it housed some type of support equipment for the main building, which had been sold to the city of Farmington as a sports arena and events facility that would eventually be second to none.

Though he found it hard to imagine in the sunny Southwest, one of the much-discussed future residents of this facility was rumored to be a professional hockey team. That was of course assuming it was ever completed – the project had been more than a decade in the making now, and the budget was still growing, even as the timetable stretched out to the horizon. Looking at the sheer size of the building, even with refrigeration equipment, parking, storage, and who knows *what* else, it looked as though it would still have room for at *least* 50 zambonis. Perhaps 100! For any city, particularly a smallish former oil town in the Southwest, it struck Luke as overkill. In fact, the very idea of the facility, not just the hockey dreams, but even the promise of luring an NBA team, it all struck him as rather pie in the sky. While the rest of Farmington had bought into the much-delayed project, Luke, who had only been back in the area

for a year now, watched it all from a cynic's point
of view. Every time the project's mastermind and
ostensible figurehead came to the city to ask for more
money, or more time, the hairs on the back of Luke's
neck bristled.

The crowd murmured with excitement as Jake
Dupuis, a successful 62 year-old developer, who
had long ago been the star quarterback for the
Farmington High School football team, and who
still walked with a bit of that "big man on campus"
swagger, in spite of two bum knees and a few extra
pounds, emerged on stage. With a solid build and a
thick grey beard, Dupuis remained a highly visible
figure in Farmington, where four decades on he
was still using that high school athlete influence to
finesse profitable business partnerships around town.
As with so many people in the area, the economic
troubles over the last few years had not been easy
on him, but he'd gotten by, largely, it seemed, by
hitching his wagon to the promise of Ben Gerritt's
long-delayed sports complex on the outskirts of
Chokecherry Canyon.

People clapped softly as Dupuis nodded and
smiled. Then Ben Gerritt, 70 years old, looking fit,
muscular, and thin as a whip, bounded up on stage
beside him. *That's* when the crowd went wild. If Jacob
Dupuis was a local hero, Ben Gerritt, with his steely
gaze, deeply lined face, and silver hair, was a living

legend. Under his signature black cowboy hat, Gerritt strongly resembled a latter-day Clint Eastwood. A longtime player in area politics and commerce, Gerritt was playing a role he knew all too well, one that fit him like a second skin. As the largest backer of the arena, and by default the unofficial civic leader behind the project, he was both a booster for the dream and the man poised to make the most money from the enterprise if it proved successful.

Gerritt had played the part of the concerned booster with a little skin in the game countless times over the past forty years, initially as mayor, and later as a public figure, pushing for a bigger college, the construction of the downtown civic center, development of Chokecherry Canyon, and of course, doing anything he could to boost oil and gas exploration in the area. *That* was where the bulk of his substantial personal fortune had originated. After a fairly long retreat from the public eye, when he reemerged as the face and virtual engine driving the arena project forward, it had quickly become Ben Gerritt's biggest and most elaborate project *ever*, and after a decade-long push to bring it to fruition, today marked his first public appearance since the complex had finally begun to take shape. He was clearly enjoying the attention, grinning and bowing and waving to the crowd like a dyed-in-the-wool politician, which was another part he'd played over the years, but that was another matter...

"Ladies and gentlemen..." Dupuis called through the public address system as the clapping and hollering continued. "Ladies and gentlemen... As you all know, I am very proud to be involved in the construction of Ben Gerritt's *fabulous* new arena!"

The crowd once more went nuts, and Dupuis turned to Gerritt, the two of them flashing grins like a couple of fat cats who'd just divvied up one very plump canary backstage.

"The arena, like the man who has worked tirelessly to make it a reality over all these years, is certain to provide a lifetime of entertainment, service, and *revenue* to this great city."

Luke clapped his hands with measured enthusiasm, watching Red Sanders from the corner of his eye to gauge the older man's reaction to everything. Red was smiling, but he looked like a man who was mentally reviewing his grocery list as he went through the motions of his workday. So far, the presentation was boilerplate, but the audience was eating it up.

Luke looked around the crowd, wondering what had brought so many of them out today to serve largely as a backdrop for Ben Gerritt's latest victory lap. He supposed they just loved the guy, and they were pinning their financial hopes on his next big idea. Maybe it was from all his years away, but instinctively, Luke didn't share their enthusiasm. He was skeptical, he was dubious, and he was just about to suggest breakfast at TJ's Diner, when his eyes locked on a woman three rows ahead of them. Her brownish red hair was pulled back in a ponytail. She was a little thinner than the last time he'd seen her – which had been at *least* ten years ago – but there was no mistaking Carley Parker. Luke watched closely as she jotted down notes in a small notebook.

"And now, it is my distinct honor to present to you a great man, and my good friend, former *Mayor* Ben Gerritt!"

Dupuis swept his arm towards Gerritt, who stepped forward, a relaxed, almost sheepish smile crossing his face. The two men shook hands and slapped one another on the back, really playing up the old friends routine. Then Gerritt stepped up to the lectern, nodding and smiling as he waited for the rumble of the crowd to settle down.

"Thank you. Thank you. And thank you to Jake, for that kind introduction." Gerritt clapped his hands together. "Jake Dupuis, quarterback for *three seasons of championship Farmington football!*," Gerritt bellowed as he worked the crowd into a frenzy again. "Tough act to follow. Tough act to follow."

The audience laughed as Jake Dupuis took a few exaggerated bows, and Gerritt waited for just the right moment to speak.

"But seriously folks, I don't want to keep you out here too long. I really appreciate your enthusiasm. This is quite an honor. I know how hard times have been for many of you these last few years. This is a strong, committed, hardworking community. When I first proposed this center way back... back..." Gerritt paused and laughed and the audience chuckled with him. "Well, I cringe to *think* how long ago it was. I was simply looking for a way to bring business and money back to this city after our traditional industries had fallen on hard times. I never imagined things would get as tough for everyone out here as they have these last few years. And I never dreamed this little dream of mine would take on such personal importance. But it has. Believe me."

The crowd ate that up too, hooting and hollering as Gerritt smiled again. Luke clapped along halfheartedly as he stood up straight and tried to get a better look at Carley.

"I'm not one for big speeches, so I'll get to the point. As far as I'm concerned, the Gerritt Arena, which, by the way, that name is such an honor, such an honor... The Gerritt Arena is *more* than just a sports complex, it's *more* than just a place for the hardworking people of this city to come and see a basketball game, or catch a concert, and yes, despite the naysayers, maybe even watch some hockey. To me it's a symbol of what's next for Farmington.

We're about to embark on the next step in this city's illustrious history." He paused as the people in attendance roared their approval and cheered his name." We're going to show people throughout the state and throughout the Southwest that Farmington isn't just *in* the game, it's *winning* the game. We're going to lead the pack, lead the state, and hell, we're going to give people all over the *country* a run for their money. The arena is Farmington's next big step! We're going to be bigger, better, more successful, and more *inspiring* than ever! Let's make Farmington *great* again!"

Gerritt was all grins as the applause drowned him out entirely now. He started to take a step back, but Jake Dupuis came forward holding a giant pair of scissors. Gerritt slapped himself on the forehead as though he'd forgotten.

Luke's lip curled at the good-old-boy atmosphere as Dupuis stepped forward, handed off the scissors, and Gerritt snipped the red ribbon that was stretched across the front of the stage. Luke watched the crowd up ahead and tipped his head from side to side, trying to get a better look at Carley. Suddenly, she spun around and looked him right in the eyes. She cracked a smile and the years fell away. At 32 years of age, Luke's long-ago high school sweetheart was as beautiful as ever. He nodded hello.

"You getting this?" Red asked as he nudged Luke

with his elbow.

Carley pointed at Gerritt and Dupuis and held up her camera.

So, she was working at her father's paper!

"I said you getting this, Luke," Red repeated.

"Oh, yeah, *yeah,*" Luke answered.

He hoisted his own camera and snapped off a couple of pictures as Gerritt lowered the scissors and put his hand on Jake Dupuis' shoulder. Then Dupuis stepped forward and spoke into the microphone.

"Now, for those of you who can make it, we'd be honored if you could join us for a special reception at the country club. Members of the media, this is your chance to get those exclusive Ben Gerritt sound bytes we know you all love so much."

"That's our cue," Red whispered in Luke's ear. "Can you give me a ride over there as well?"

Luke watched as Carley disappeared into the crowd.

"Sure thing, boss," he replied.

Hopefully, Carley Parker would be there as well.

***

Mick Gridley walked sleepily down the police station corridor, a steaming dose of bitter, overcooked coffee burning through the paper cup he was holding. He passed the scalding beverage from one hand to the other, dreading the next step, but craving the caffeine, even as he anticipated the smoldering hole the first sip would tear through his stomach. He rounded the corner and strolled into the crime lab, where a bushy-haired lab worker was hunched over a computer.

"Hey, Jason. You have a minute?" Gridley asked.

Jason Croatto was one of the few folks Mick had encountered in the Farmington Police Department who spoke to him unguardedly. Whereas everyone else seemed to be withholding even the most routine information when he queried them, Croatto always offered candid, reliable information.

"What can I do for you, Mick?" Jason asked.

"You get anything from the crime scene last night?"

"Well, like we expected, nothing from the knife handle. Pouch's things are still bagged and waiting in that crate over there." He nodded in the direction of a large, sealed, plastic bin sitting on a stainless steel table across the room. "If we're lucky, we might have some of the fingerprint and DNA analysis back this afternoon."

Gridley rubbed his chin as he pulled out his pen and notebook. He wasn't expecting anything terribly helpful to come from the lab analysis anyway. He walked over to the container and pulled off the top.

"You got some gloves I can use?"

"Under the table."

Gridley pulled on a pair of latex gloves and returned to the container. He pulled out Pouch's wallet, flipped it open, and copied the dead man's address off his driver's license. Then he felt through the pockets of Pouch's bloody coat till he found a cell phone. He looked the phone over carefully, flipped it open, and glanced over at Croatto. After a moment's hesitation, he hit the REDIAL button. The phone rang a couple of times before a voice came on the line.

"Good morning, Dupuis Construction," a friendly female voice said.

Gridley cut the call short.

Croatto looked up from his computer, then turned, and went back to his work.

***

Luke stood at the top of a half-flight of stairs, looking out across the banquet hall to a wall of windows that provided a view of the country club's golf course. The grass on the fairway was a wintry shade of khaki, but even then, he could see a pair of golfers out playing a round in the mild air. Inside, a crowd of the city's biggest movers and shakers milled about, making small talk and sipping cocktails.

Luke was tired as hell. And he saw no necessity for this reception in the first place. Despite Jake Dupuis' all-inclusive invite, the event was really only intended for select individuals from the media, a handful of the city's well-to-do, and anyone else who had greased the skids in helping the arena project gain momentum over the years. Still, it was approaching lunchtime, and the event *did* have sandwiches and an open bar, so he decided to make the most of it. Luke descended the stairs and walked over to the buffet, where he loaded a plate with two cross-sections of a ten-foot Italian sub, grabbed a stool at the bar, and took a bite.

The bartender approached, polishing the countertop, as Luke swallowed his first bite of sandwich.

"What can I get for you?"

"If you have the ingredients, I'll take a white Russian," Luke replied.

The bartender gave him a quick nod as he set a thick crystal glass on the counter, filled it with a scoop of ice, simultaneously poured in two generous portions of Kahlua and vodka, topped it off with cream and a swizzle stick, and slid the drink down the bar.

Luke reached into his pocket for a tip.

The bartender raised his hand. "Thanks, but it's covered."

"Are you sure?"

"Couldn't take it if I wanted to. Against club rules."

"Well, thank you," Luke said as he swirled the drink layers together.

The bartender smiled and walked away.

Luke took a sip and looked around the room. The crowd had begun to dissipate. Red had disappeared into a smoking lounge with a couple of producers from the local network affiliates. Jake Dupuis and Ben Gerritt were working the room, glad-handing anyone who came up to them. Luke felt a tap on his shoulder.

"How's it going, stranger?"

He turned to see Carley Parker smiling beside him.

"Hey. I was hoping I might run into you here," he said.

"I was hoping to get a chance to talk to Ben Gerritt."

"And did you?"

"Not yet, but maybe if I sit with someone from his own paper, I'll stand a better chance. I assume you're back working for *The Times* again?"

"You assume correctly."

"I didn't realize you'd moved back to town," Carley said.

"Same to you. Last I heard you were in... Albuquerque?"

Carley nodded. "And I think you were someplace in Upstate New York."

"Rochester."

"Rochester. Doesn't it snow six months out of the

year up there?"

"It's not quite that bad, but it sure feels like it sometimes. Mostly it's just spine-crackingly cold."

"Well, the cold must keep you young. You look good."

Luke laughed. "You're being kind. But you, *you* look great."

Her cheeks flushed. "Thanks."

"I heard a rumor you were married."

"I *was* married."

"What are you now?"

She took a drink of water, crunching an ice cube in her teeth before she answered. "I'm in sort of a... holding pattern."

"OK then, next subject!" Luke motioned to the camera around her neck in an effort to change course. "So, where are you working?"

"At *The Aztec Review*. I took over from my Dad when he retired."

"Ohh, the competition... Maybe I shouldn't be spotted with you."

"Maybe you *shouldn't*. Gerritt does still own your paper, right?"

"He does."

Luke took a sip of his drink and looked across the room. Red had re-emerged from the smoking room and was now talking with Ben Gerritt.

Luke turned back to Carley and nodded at the

39

bartender. "You want something to drink, Carley?"

"I might grab a sandwich for the road. Little early for me to hit the sauce though."

"You're probably smarter than I am," Luke said. "But I had a *really* long night, so I'm making an exception. How'd you like that ham bone routine at the ceremony?"

'Distinctly Farmington," Carley said. "Distinctly Ben Gerritt. He knows what he's doing, though. Everyone loves him."

"That they do." Luke agreed. "Let me ask you something. Do you ever get the feeling he's fixing to run for office again?"

"I don't know," She replied, taking on a conspiratorial tone. "He does seem to be upping his profile lately. Maybe he's thinking of something after the arena. He had kind of dropped off the map for a long while. I've never really heard anything about why that was exactly."

"Me neither. But if you recall your Farmington history, he resigned as mayor pretty abruptly back in the day. He dropped off the map then too, but no one around town ever talks about that."

"Any idea what made him do it?" she asked.

"Resign? I have no idea. I *do* know what he did afterward though, 'cause my old man went to work for him. From government to oil and gas. 1-2-3. Your typical story around here."

"I was sorry to hear he'd passed. Your father, I mean."

"Oh, thanks. At least it wasn't unexpected. He was in rough shape for a long time. Actually, the reason I came back to town was to help him out as best I could."

"I always liked him."

"He always liked *you*."

They sat quietly for a moment, eating their food and grasping for conversation.

"How did your father like working for Ben Gerritt?"

"He didn't," Luke answered without a moment's hesitation. "Dad didn't think too highly of Gerritt. Even after he started his own mud-logging business, he never had much nice to say about old Ben."

A hand dropped on his shoulder and Luke jumped slightly, turning to see Red standing beside him. Red waved a hand toward Ben Gerritt, who towered over the three of them.

"Luke," Red said. "I believe you know the Mayor."

Luke made eye contact with Carley, but quickly looked away.

He hoped like hell neither of them had heard what he and Carley had been saying.

"Ben, this is Mike Murphy's boy. He's been back in town for the last year, working for us at *The Times*."

Ben Gerritt studied Luke for a split second, then

a smile snapped into place and he put out his hand.

"Listen to this guy. One of the few folks around town who *still* calls me 'Mayor.' I love it! Of course I remember Murphy's boy. Luke, good to see you again." Gerritt looked at Luke's half-finished drink. "White Russian. A man after my own heart, I see." He caught the bartender's attention. "I'll have one of those as well."

"Luke was at the scene last night when they found Harvey Pouch," Red added.

"Oh yeah?" Gerritt asked absentmindedly as he watched the bartender repeat the process of fixing the drink.

A layer of Kahlua. A layer of vodka. Topped off with cream.

The bartender slid the glass across the bar. Luke watched as Gerritt removed the unused swizzle stick, set it on the counter, and took a sip. The Kahlua stayed at the bottom of the glass, so the first sip was mostly cream.

Gerritt saw him watching.

"I like the layers. Take things as they come."

Luke nodded, but something about the gesture struck him as quite odd. He tried to come up with something to say in response, and finally turned to Carley.

"Mr. Gerritt, this is my old friend Carley Parker, from *The Aztec Review.*"

Gerritt took another sip of his drink, gently rocking the glass as he shook Carley's hand. He once again turned on the charm.

"Oh, the competition. Ms. Parker, pleasure to meet you."

"Likewise, Mr. Gerritt."

"Carley was hoping she might get an interview with you," Luke said.

"Oh really?"

"Nothing big,"Carley said. "I just have a few questions about the center."

Gerritt took another slug of his drink. By now, he was down to the vodka and Kahlua, which he threw back in one final gulp. He wiped his mouth with a cocktail napkin and looked over at a man in a dark suit, who was standing at the top of the stairs. The man turned their way, and Gerritt nodded to him.

"Normally, I'd hate to risk giving a rival publication any sort of scoop," Gerritt said as he got to his feet. "But I want to give this arena all the coverage it can get. And for a lovely young woman like yourself, I'm more than happy to make an exception. Unfortunately, I'm afraid I'm a little short on time today, but if you call my office, my assistant can make you an appointment."

"That would be great," Carley said.

"Sorry to cut this short."

"Don't be silly," Red said. "You're a busy man, Mr. Mayor. I'll walk you out."

"Folks, have a great afternoon." Gerritt shook hands all around and headed for the stairs with Red at his side.

Carley turned her head and locked eyes with Luke. He knew from her expression that something had struck her as very odd. He waited until Gerritt and Red had reached the top of the stairs, then he arched his eyebrows to see what was up.

"That was bizarre," Carley whispered.

"What?"

"Gerritt. When Red mentioned Harvey Pouch, there was no reaction whatsoever."

"What did you expect him to do, break down sobbing?"

"Maybe not sobbing, but *some* sort of response wouldn't have been out of the question given the circumstances, you know?"

Luke picked up his glass, rubbing his thumb over the perspiration beading on the sides.

"I wish I could say I did, but I'm afraid I'm not following you."

"You really don't know what I'm talking about?"

Luke shook his head.

"Luke, Harvey Pouch was Ben Gerritt's son-in-law."

"You're kidding me!"

"Do you remember Melanie Gerritt?"

"Remember her? Every guy in *town* remembers her. I had *dreams* about that girl."

"Well, I could have done without hearing *that*," Carley said with a laugh. "At any rate, Harvey Pouch is the guy she married. It lasted about ten years, and from what I've heard, she was never around for any of it."

"And why was that exactly?" Luke asked.

"I don't think personal affection ever played a part in the whole arrangement, if you know what I mean. People I know figure Gerritt pushed her into marrying him. Pouch was actually *successful* back then. He was involved in a lot of businesses with Jake Dupuis. Melanie Gerritt took the vow, enjoyed his money, and spent ten years traveling. When Pouch went broke, she came back, got a divorce, and took the party somewhere back East."

"In good times and in bad, huh?"

"Not where the Gerritt family is concerned I guess. But still, wouldn't you have expected Gerritt to have *some* sort of reaction? He didn't so much as blink."

"He's an unusual guy. I've never known what to make of him."

"But like you said, your dad didn't like him."

"No, he certainly did not."

Luke took a sip of his drink and surveyed the room. He happened to look over just as Sonny West walked into the banquet hall with a couple of off-duty police officers. Sonny was dressed casually, as were the two guys with him. Luke recognized one of them from the crime scene the previous night.

"What day is this anyways?" Luke asked Carley.

"Friday."

"I didn't realize so many cops were off the clock on weekdays."

She followed his gaze till she saw who he was looking at and rolled her eyes. "With him, that doesn't surprise me in the least."

Sonny and his buddies took a seat at the far end of the bar. He looked over and saw Luke and Carley sitting at the other end.

"Hey Murphy!" Sonny called as he got back to his feet.

"Christ," Luke muttered under his breath. He looked up and put on the broadest smile he could force, as Sonny walked up and put out his hand. "Hey, Sonny, what's up?"

"Not a whole hell of a lot." He looked at Carley and gave her a wink. "Carley Parker. As I live and breathe. It has been a *while.*"

Carley's lip started to curl involuntarily. Sonny was clearly not one of her favorite people.

"Yeah. It's been a while," she replied with a sharp nod. "How are you, Sonny?"

Sonny shrugged. "Eh, you know. I'm keeping on." He directed his attention back to Luke. "Luke buddy, I was gonna call you. My softball team is looking for a new pitcher."

"Oh yeah...?" Luke was skeptical. With Sonny there was always an angle or a punch line waiting around the corner.

"You still got it man? I haven't seen you on the field since high school."

"I haven't *been* on the field since high school."

"Well, you gotta get back out there then! Come to one of our practices. I think we could use you."

"Thanks for the offer," Luke demurred, "but I'm happily retired from the game."

Sonny smacked him on the back. "Come on man. Carley, you saw him play back in high school! Tell this guy he's wasting his talent."

"Luke. You're wasting your talent," she said in as monotone a voice as possible.

"Thanks," Sonny deadpanned. "You're a real help. But I'm serious, man, tell me you'll think about it."

"O.K. I'll think about it, Sonny."

Sonny set his hand on Luke's shoulder.

"That's all that I ask," he said before he headed back to the far end of the bar to rejoin his buddies.

"Same old Sonny," Luke muttered softly.

Carley shook her head and smiled. "You're not really going to think about it, are you?"

"God no."

~

Luke and Carley strolled out of the country club and into the parking lot. The afternoon sun had broken through the clouds. Carley pulled on a pair of sunglasses as Luke shielded his eyes with one hand.

"Can I give you a lift?" he asked

"Oh, thanks, but I'm good." She pointed to a bright yellow car at the end of the nearest row. "The VW at the end is mine." She reached over and set her hand on his forearm. "It was good to see you, Luke."

He looked smitten. "Good to see you, too. Keep in touch, will you?"

She brushed her hair out of her eyes as she started for her car. "I'll do that."

***

Luke sat at his desk that afternoon, once more staring down into his mug of coffee. He should have written up a recap of the arena ceremony by now. Actually, he should have gone home and gotten some sleep, then come back and written up an article, but his mind kept wandering back to Carley.

He glanced over at a post-it note on the side of his monitor, where he'd written down the number for *The Aztec Review*. He was trying to come up with a good excuse to give her a ring, maybe under the guise of checking a quote or something, even if the two of them knew all too well that it was a bogus excuse to get back in touch. Finally, he leaned forward, grabbed the post-it and his phone and headed for the front door. If he was going to call her, he sure as hell wasn't going to do it within earshot of anyone on the news floor.

He was just passing the front counter when Grace held a slip of paper out for him. "Luke, I almost forgot, after you finish the arena piece, Red phoned in an assignment for you."

Luke took the paper, a look of confusion passing over his face as he read it over.

"*Gleiberman?* What is this?"

"Owen Gleiberman, he's on the high school baseball team. The coach has a rule about long hair. He doesn't allow it to hang below the ear. This kid Gleiberman doesn't want to cut his."

"OK," Luke said slowly. "But... what's the story?"

"The story is that it's causing a mini-controversy over at the high school, plus the kid's father is one of Mayor Griffin's golf buddies."

Luke rolled his eyes. "Only in a small town. Ridiculous."

"Yes, it is," she replied, "But it's also your assignment. Red wants to run an interview by Monday."

Luke sighed and slipped the paper into his pocket as he continued for the door. "Have a good one, Grace," he grumbled.

***

Luke dug through the freezer, debating which Stouffer's creation he would release from suspended animation tonight. He settled on the pizza, tearing the shrink-wrap from the frosty pie as he crossed the kitchen and preheated the oven.

He glanced at his cell phone, next to which he'd placed the number for *The Aztec Review*. He hadn't tried Carley at the office, because really, work would not have been the reason for his call. If she was busy at her father's old paper, and if she *was* back in town after being gone for so many years, he had a sneaking suspicion she was staying at her childhood home for the time being. He knew *that* number by heart.

Still, there was a lot to consider before he gave her a call on a strictly social pretense. There was a lot of history to delve into, and some of it wasn't so pleasant.

Then again... a lot of it was.

Unfortunately, he still didn't know what exactly her situation was. Maybe she was still married. But he hadn't seen a ring on her finger today. The thing was, he knew a bit more about her marriage than he had let on today. Farmington was a relatively small community, and the thing with small towns is that even after someone leaves, they still hear stories about old friends and associates, and how things have panned out for them. The web of small town connections is tight-knit and long-lasting, no matter where you end up.

He knew secondhand a bit of the history between Carley and her estranged or ex-husband. He knew about the domestic violence charges, the numerous separations, and the heart-breaking pattern of returning to Albuquerque to give it another go. The fact that she had been back in the area for more than six months was a good sign. A very good sign. But he wasn't quite sure if he was ready to see if there was still anything there.

The oven beeped that it was ready. Luke pulled open the door and tossed the unwrapped pizza on the bare rack. He could hear the crust sizzling on the hot metal as he shut the door and headed into the living room. KOB news was running their report on the arena ceremony. Footage of Gerritt cutting the ribbon and working the crowd played as the announcer added his commentary.

"With the economy grinding through the most punishing recession in generations, Ben Gerritt appeared before an eager crowd of onlookers with their hopes pinned to the long-delayed complex. Everyone involved is hoping what's good for the center will be good for Farmington. Aside from professional sports and a wish list of musical acts, the new complex is set to house numerous shops, office spaces, and dining options, a combination Gerritt believes will inject new life into the local economy."

The coverage switched to interviews with people in the audience. Luke switched off the TV and headed back into the kitchen, where he grabbed the garbage and headed out the door. If he hadn't been so distracted, he'd have taken the time to peek out the window to make sure the coast was clear.

It wasn't.

No sooner did he toss the bag in the dumpster across the parking lot and head back into the apartment complex's courtyard, than he saw the all too familiar figure of Margo Fisher, 40 years-old, with a thick wave of red hair, leopard print tights that fit her legs like a second skin, and a baggy pink sweater, standing in the middle of the doorway across from his, recording his every movement with a tiny video camera. The smoking nub of a cigarette poked up between her fingers. Her five year-old son hung at her legs, peanut butter caked to his face as he watched Luke with a hangdog expression.

"*Smile...*" Margo called over to him suggestively. "You're on Candid Camera."

Luke's shoulders drew up in panic as he grimaced. He turned around slowly, trying to think his way out of this one, even as he struggled to suppress his flight instinct and deliver a four-word sentence.

"You got me, Margo."

"Not where I want you," Margo said with a wink. "How you doing, neighbor?

She lowered the camera, contorting her body in an alarming attempt to appear seductive.

Luke ran his fingers over the door key in his fingers. His palms were sweating.

"Ohhh... I'm doing okay..".

"Hard day?" she asked.

Luke eyed his door.

"No, not too bad really."

"Care to come in, have some coffee? I could show you some...home movies."

"You know what? I have a pizza in the oven. I better go check on that."

"Did you set the buzzer?"

"I did."

"Well, I haven't heard any bells? Have you?"

"No," Luke muttered. "No I haven't. But I probably ought to head in. I need to get to bed early. Get some extra sleep."

"Now, what do you want to do that for? There are much better things you could being doing other than sleeping."

Luke gulped.

His mind was racing, tripping over possible excuses as he tried to plot his escape. Then he heard something. It wasn't the timer for the oven, but it was the next best thing. His cellphone was ringing.

"Oh, that's for me," Luke said as he walked backward, like an animal trainer, afraid to turn his back on a lion.

"Ta-ta." Margo replied, giving him another slow

wink as he closed the door behind him.

Luke leaned the back of his head against the front door, catching his breath for a moment, relieved to be inside again.

The phone!

He hurried across the room and answered his phone.

"Hello?" he said into the handset.

"Yes, I'm looking for Luke Murphy. From *The Daily Times?*"

Luke didn't recognize the voice.

"I'm sorry," Luke answered. "But who may I ask is calling?"

"This is Mick Gridley," the voice replied. "We met last night. I'm the lead detective on the Pouch murder."

"Oh right. Hi. How are you?"

"Frankly, I'm a little suspicious at the moment. Let me give you an address. There's just been a fire at Harvey Pouch's place."

3.

Fire trucks were scattered around the smoldering hulk of what had once been Harvey Pouch's home on the bluffs outside town. Even in ruins, Luke could see the evidence of Harvey's one-time success. It must have been an enormous place. Now, aside from the grounds, which were largely unscathed, all that was left of the massive home was the charred skeleton of the wooden framing. Luke peered through his camera's viewfinder, framing a shot of the firefighters directing a stream of water back and forth across the remains. He lowered the camera and surveyed the hazy scene.

Christ. He hoped he'd turned off the oven before he left.

Luke bit his lip as he watched the expressions of the scattered onlookers in the crowd. Then, for the umpteenth time in the last 24 hours, he saw Sonny West walking toward him.

"We've gotta stop meeting like this," Sonny said.

"Where's Detective Gridley?"

Sonny pointed to the back of the property, where

Gridley was just walking around to the corner of the house. Sonny's handheld radio made a squawking noise as a voice broke through the static. Sonny pulled the handset to his ear and walked away from the crowd.

Luke headed toward Gridley.

The detective looked up, clearing his throat when he saw him. "Hell of a mess, huh?" He looked back at the house, just as a thick cloud of steam billowed over them. "Pouch had his office in the front of the house. Can you guess where the fire originated?"

"The front?"

"Bingo."

"When did it start?" Luke asked.

Gridley pointed to a house on the hill across the road. A family was gathered on the front lawn. Their dog was running around in circles, barking up at the sky.

"Neighbors called it in around 9 o'clock." Gridley lowered his voice and started walking toward the edge of the property, motioning for Luke to follow him. "Fire made short work of the place. I can't imagine the fire investigator will turn up much for me to work with."

Luke and Gridley had walked a short distance from the crowd now, and the detective lowered his head, dropping his voice to a murmur as he spoke.

"Lemme ask you something," Gridley began. "Do you feel as though there's something strange going on here?"

"Are you asking me as a reporter?" Luke asked warily.

"Just in general. I'm the new guy around here, so I'm not sure how people usually act around this type of scene, at least not in *this* department. I couldn't help but notice that you have a little rapport with Sonny, but some of the other guys, if you don't mind my saying so, seemed to treat you like shit at the crime scene last night. And you're a *local*, right?"

"Technically, yeah, I suppose I am. But I was away from Farmington for a *long* time. As far as some of the guys on the force are concerned, I think that makes me a bit... suspect now."

"That's the impression I was getting." Gridley nodded. "And that's why I'm asking. Because to me, Harvey Pouch's home burning down the *day* after he's murdered, in a fire that clearly originated in his office no less, *that* strikes me as more than a coincidence." Gridley was just about whispering now. "But the way people in this department are acting whenever I raise questions, it makes me think they're either completely uninterested in this case, or they don't *want* to know what's going on. It's like they're afraid to know the truth. That to me seems to indicate there's something more going on here."

Luke looked confused. He glanced back at the crowd of firefighters and police officers. "Help me out here," he whispered. "What are you getting at?"

"Warning bells are going off in the back of my head," Gridley said. "Is there a place we can get a drink?"

~

If there was one bar in the city that guaranteed as few eavesdroppers as possible, it was the Skyliner at the Farmington Airport. Ever since regular flights in and out of the area had been rerouted through Albuquerque, the small, but once-steadily busy airport had been reduced to a watering hole for the city's well-to-do, who owned their own planes and either had their pilots' licenses, or could afford to keep pilots on staff. With the airport largely abandoned, the once-bustling Mexican restaurant and cantina had been reduced to a hangout for pilots, daytime drinkers, and folks looking to eat and drink without their get-togethers winding up in the gossip circles about town.

Luke came here for the solitude, and because the bartender, Rene, made an exceptional white Russian; they had a sort of butterscotch aftertaste that he could never seem to pin down. And though he'd been watching Rene fix them for almost a year, they *seemed* to be made with the usual ingredients. It must have been something in the cream. Perhaps somewhere in Farmington, a dairy cow was getting butterscotch discs with her daily meals. That was the best he could come up with.

"Mother's milk?" Rene asked Luke the moment he and Gridley took a seat in the corner booth.

"Sure," Luke replied.

Mother's milk was some sort of odd joke Rene liked to deploy whenever Luke ordered his signature drink. Luke had asked him to explain the line once, but it turned out it was something one of his regulars at another bar had said years ago when ordering the same beverage. Apparently it was *that* patron's favorite as well, and though the guy evidently had a strange sense of humor, he clearly had good taste when it came to cocktails.

"What the hell is *'mother's milk?'*" Gridley asked.

Rene turned and looked at Luke, cracking a little grin as he waited for him to field the question.

How in the hell had that wisecrack gotten pinned on him?!

"It's a long story," Luke sighed. "They're good."

"In that case, make that two." Gridley said.

"Any food?" Rene asked as he tapped the menus on the edge of the table.

"Yeah, I might take a look," Luke replied.

Rene set the menus on the table and headed back to the bar.

"What exactly did I just order?" Gridley asked, once

the bartender was out of earshot.

"A white Russian."

"Oh, those aren't bad!"

"Wait 'til you have Rene's." Luke said. He looked around the room to be sure the place was empty. "Can you talk now? What's this about?"

Gridley leaned forward, still speaking in a hushed tone, but loud enough that Luke could hear him comfortably. "So, you know I'm new to this department, right?"

Luke nodded.

"Now, I don't know how things work here. But it's a hell of a lot different than it was in Seattle."

"How so?"

"I just get this strange feeling here. Like..." he trailed off.

"Like what?" Luke arched his eyebrows expectantly.

"Like I'm not getting any cooperation on things," Gridley continued. "It's been this way since day one, but recently it's gotten much more pronounced. Take the Pouch murder, and the fire tonight. If I didn't know better, I'd assume no one who showed up at either of those scenes, last night *or* today, gave a shit about getting to the bottom of what had gone down. Asking even the most benign questions seems to make them uncomfortable. They act like doing anything might stir up trouble."

"By 'them,' do you mean people in the

department?"

Gridley nodded.

"Look, maybe I shouldn't be saying anything, but this isn't the first time I've felt it. And I don't think its just because I'm the new guy. This afternoon I applied for a warrant to search Harvey Pouch's house. It was supposed to clear by tomorrow morning. Now here we are a few hours later, and any possible evidence just went up in smoke."

Rene returned with their drinks. The other good thing about Rene's white Russians: He always mixed them. None of the layered nonsense like the bartender at the country club had pulled that afternoon. Luke took a sip and mulled what Gridley was suggesting.

"So let me ask you something," Luke said as he set down his glass. "Why are you opening up to me about this? Aren't you afraid I'll go talk to Sonny, or someone else that could just turn around and put the squeeze on you?"

Mick looked at him for a moment, double checking his gut. "I don't think you will. 'Cause I get the sense you know exactly what I'm getting at. I'm new to small towns, but people are people wherever you end up. The crooks always stick together, until they don't. And guys like you and me see through all of 'em. Am I right, or am I right?"

Luke cracked a smile. "You lost me a little, but I

think you give me more credit than I deserve."

"Maybe so, but you didn't disagree with me either."

"Ok, so then lets drill down, shall we? What are you telling me, that the guy who killed Harvey Pouch also burned down his house to cover his tracks?"

Maybe not the *exact* same guy, but even if it was more than one person, I'm betting the two incidents are related."

Luke shrugged. "That would make sense to me."

Gridley stared at his drink, deliberating, then he reached down and took a drink. "Damn. This *is* good."

"I told you so," Luke said. "Well, since we're sharing, let me tell you what *I* learned about Harvey Pouch today. It's only in the last ten years that he's been broke. Before that, the guy was apparently in the money. You know Jake Dupuis?"

"No."

"He's a big developer in town. His company has built half the city. He's sort of a small-town hero-"

"Wait a minute!" Gridley blurted out. "Yeah. *Dupuis Construction.* That was the number on Pouch's phone."

"His phone?"

"There's one guy in the lab who doesn't seem hell-bent on keeping me away from anything that might yield something along the lines of a *clue.* I was going through Pouch's things from the murder scene and happened to hit redial on his cell phone. Dupuis Construction was the last place he called."

"Well that's interesting. They're the ones building the new arena I was covering today too."

"That must be a sweet contract."

Luke nodded his head emphatically, splashing white Russian as he took a sip. He lowered the glass and wiped his lip. "From what I gather, Pouch and Dupuis were in business together years ago."

"And how did that end? Amicably?"

"*That* I'm still working to figure out."

"I'll look into it, too," Gridley mused, wiping away a milk moustache. "Now, is the food here as good as their drinks?"

***

Luke took a detour on his way home, driving toward the outskirts of town, but turning at the last moment and hopping on the new stretch of highway that had been constructed through the middle of Chokecherry Canyon in the years he was living back East.

When he was a kid, this area had been desert. Nothing but sandstone bluffs and a dried-up riverbed. Now, as he drove though the cool night air, he had a clear view of the backs of the neighborhoods he'd ridden his dirt bike through as a kid. Lights were on in most of the houses. The blue glow from televisions flickered in the windows. He wondered how many of these places were still owned by the parents of his childhood classmates. As in many small towns, people had come and gone over the years, but for most folks in Farmington, the idea of ever moving away was inconceivable.

His father had been one of those people.

Farmington-born and raised, Mike Murphy had worked there all his life, taking odd jobs in his youth, before eventually moving into the oil business. He began by working on drilling rigs, before eventually going back to school and branching out into the mud-logging business, where he helped investors pinpoint the places they were most likely to locate oil or natural gas. At different points in his life, usually when he'd been drinking too much and too often, his old man had found himself working for Ben Gerritt, in any number of capacities. He'd actually been on the verge of going back to work for the man one last time, right up until the day he died. In a way, though he never said why, Luke got the impression that for Mike Murphy, the idea of once more working for Farmington's one-time mayor would have been a fate worse than death. For that reason, if for nothing else, Luke was almost relieved his old man had been spared that final indignity.

Luke studied the rows of houses again. His eyes drifted a short distance away, where they locked on the darkened silhouette of a tall home set off by itself. None of the windows in that house were illuminated. No one had been inside for close to a year. Luke studied the dark shape a moment longer before he reached over and turned on the radio, hoping to drown out his thoughts. He cranked up the volume and stepped on the gas.

~

Luke played back his messages as he helped himself to another drink. He was about to take his first sip when Carley's voice came on the speaker and he froze in his tracks.

"Luke, its Carley. I have some interesting information to pass along. Give me a call when you get in."

He lifted his glass and glanced at the number on the caller ID. If he'd looked at it first, he'd have known right away that she was indeed living at her father's place again. He debated calling her right back, but told himself it was too late.

Besides, he wanted an excuse to stop by *The Review* in person. Before work. Before anything else. He'd pick up some coffee and donuts and swing by her office first thing tomorrow morning.

~

The coffees sloshed in the cup holder as he pulled to a stop at the curb. Carley's yellow Volkswagen was parked in front of the crumbling old building, which looked almost exactly the same as it had when they were kids. Only now the walkways and the roofline looked just a bit more crooked somehow. *The Aztec Review* was and always would be the area's underdog newspaper.

Luke climbed out of his car, picked up the drinks and a box of donuts, and walked to the front windows, where he peered inside. He could see Carley sitting at a desk, typing away on a particularly dated computer. He knocked on the glass and she looked up, motioning for him to come inside.

A chime echoed in the quiet office as he opened the door and forced it closed behind him.

"How did I know you'd be working this early in the morning?" he asked.

"When you're the underdog, you've got to work *twice* as hard."

"I brought you some breakfast," Luke said, offering her one of the coffees as he stepped closer.

"Thank you," Carley said. "Underdogs need their caffeine."

"I got your message."

She took the coffee, tested it, and quickly guzzled

half the cup. "Thank you for this, by the way," she said. "I was talking to my father about the Pouch murder last night and he mentioned something else I thought you might find interesting."

"You and your father seem to have the scoop on everything!" Luke said.

"Are you ready for it?"

"Hold on." He pulled a donut from the box, offered Carley one, and took a seat across from her. "OK. Lay it on me."

"Apparently *Pouch* used to own the land on which they're building the new arena."

Luke stopped mid-bite, a halo of donut sugar circling his mouth. "You're kidding. When did he sell it?"

"Some time in the last ten years. Sold it back to the city for next to nothing. Then the city apparently turned around and sold half of it to Gerritt for even less than what they'd paid. Dad was surprised no one made a big deal about the sale."

"Aside from the obvious shadiness of the city taking an instant hit on a real estate sale, did he have anything to say about what might make it a big story?"

"I guess there was a little controversy when Pouch first bought the land twenty years ago. Ben Gerritt was mayor, and his daughter was just about to marry Pouch at the time. Gerritt was really pushing to get the sale through. It was one of the few instances where people around town were really questioning the old man's motives. Dad told me your father was very outspoken about it."

"Huh. Yeah, Dad was probably working for the city back then," Luke said. "That kind of sweetheart deal would have made his blood boil."

"That was also around the same time one of the city council members started raising questions about the way Dupuis and Pouch were closing their business deals. Guy's name was Ash Eldredge. He felt that they were getting all the city contracts because of their connections to Ben Gerritt."

"And I'm sure he was right," Luke said.

"Eldredge also started raising some financial concerns. Questioning just how much of the town's money was going into the construction jobs, and how much was going into the company's pockets."

"And how did that work out for him?"

"Eldredge? It sounds like he was starting in on a whole investigation. Wanted a big inquiry into Dupuis and Pouch, even dropped Ben Gerritt's name a few times when he spoke about it. It got in the news and was starting to get some traction. Then, out of the blue, he dropped the whole thing. Resigned his position and that was it."

Luke took out a notebook and searched around for a pen. Carley took one from a cup on her desk and tossed it to him.

"You think Mr. Eldredge had a visit from the goon squad?"

"Does Jefferson C. Pepper have more money that the royal family?" Carley asked rhetorically.

"Uh, I don't know."

"Yes, Luke. The answer is yes."

"You happen to know where I can reach this guy Eldredge? Is he still alive?"

Carley handed him a 3 X 5 card with an address and phone number.

"I'm way ahead of you. I figured you'd want to talk to him. He's expecting your call."

Luke studied the card and slipped it in his pocket. "Why are you so good to me?" he asked as he got to his feet. "In case you've forgotten, I work for a rival newspaper."

"I remember. You know I've got a soft spot for you, Luke Murphy."

"Thanks again for the information," he said as he started for the door. "Tell your father I appreciate it, too."

Back in his car, he started scanning over the pieces in his head. The hairs on the back of his neck were standing on end.

Something in the way all these disparate elements were intersecting was starting to stink.

After years of reporting on small-town crime

and politics, two subjects that crossed paths with astounding frequency, he could practically *smell* the trail of money and corruption. And wherever dirty money was concerned, Luke had learned it was usually a good idea to go in with some backup. It was never a smart idea to be the only person chasing down a lead. Hopefully, Detective Gridley would be up to joining him on this interview.

4.

Thirty minutes later, Luke and Gridley were barreling down the highway, headed for the edge of town.

"So, where did you say we're going?" Gridley asked.

Luke pointed to a piece of paper wedged beside the passenger seat. "I wrote down the directions. He said it's kinda tricky."

A short time later, Luke's beat-up Mustang crossed a small suspension bridge that passed over a dry creek. He stopped the car a short distance from a mailbox at the end of a dirt driveway. The box's red flag was up, signaling an outgoing letter was ready for pickup. A broken-down, two-story house was just visible over the pinon trees that surrounded the property. It was *not* a welcoming picture.

"*Jesus,* you think this is it?" Gridley asked.

For a cop, Gridley's voice had an unnerving quiver. Luke had brought him for protection, but Gridley sounded more nervous than *he* was!

"I don't know," Luke said as he looked over the directions. "This isn't what I was expecting."

"Can you read the name on the mailbox?"

Luke squinted. "Nah, I can't make it out. Go look inside."

"Are you serious?"

"No one can see you. Just see if there's a name on a letter or something."

"That's illegal, you know."

"Then go fast."

"I'm a cop! That's an illegal search!"

Luke looked at him in disbelief.

"Fine." Gridley hissed. *"Fine."*

He got out of the car and looked around. A lone chicken was pecking at the ground a short distance away. Gridley rushed over to the mailbox, hesitated, then pulled out a wad of letters. He was just starting to flip through them when a gunshot rang out and he practically jumped off his feet, sending, letters flying in the air.

"Jesus Christ!"

Gridley hit the deck as another shot rang out. The red flag on the mailbox exploded in a shower of sparks, pin-wheeling through the air as an old woman came tearing down the driveway a short distance away, a shotgun clasped tightly in her hands.

"Keep yer paws off my mail, you *sons of bitches!*"

Gridley raced back to the car, diving headfirst

into the passenger seat as Luke slammed his foot down on the accelerator and cranked the wheel around as far as it would go. The car kicked up gravel and dust as it fishtailed back the way it had come. The old woman was still screaming after them as they disappeared around the bend.

"Someone should go back and arrest that lunatic!" Gridley shouted as he struggled to get upright in his seat

"Why not you?" Luke asked.

"There's no way in hell I'm going back down that driveway!"

~

A few turns later, they took a right onto a roadway bookended by two sandstone pilings. The driveway was covered with tiny gravel pebbles, which kicked up under the undercarriage of the car. From his years back East, it was a sound Luke had come to associate with money. They rounded the circular driveway and pulled up in front of a low-slung home. The eaves were covered with hanging baskets full of flowers. It resembled something Frank Lloyd Wright might have designed after having an affair with Georgia O'Keeffe.

"I hope to hell we've got the right house this time," Gridley muttered.

"Yeah, this is it," Luke replied as he killed the engine

and climbed out.

The two men passed through a wrought iron gateway and headed up a tiled walkway to the covered porch. Luke rang a bell just to the side of the front entrance. A low chime murmured somewhere in the back of the home. A stained-glass window was set in the middle of the heavy wooden door, and after a few moments, a face peered out at them through the warped, multicolored glass. They could hear a heavy latch being unlocked. Then the door swung open, and they were greeted by a short, grey-haired man, who appeared to be in his early 80s.

"Mr. Eldredge?" Luke asked.

"You must be the young man from the newspaper."

"Yes I am." Luke said as he put out his hand. "Luke Murphy, from *The Times*. This is Detective Gridley, from the Farmington Police."

"Detective Gridley."

"Nice to meet you, sir," Gridley said and they politely shook hands all around. Luke noticed the way Eldredge's eyes wavered on Gridley for a moment, sizing him up.

"Pleased to meet both of you." Eldredge replied. "Please. Come in."

They followed the older man into the foyer, and waited as he closed and locked the heavy door. He led them out to a shady, covered courtyard in the middle of the home. Eldredge slowly eased his weight into a chair at the end of a weathered coffee table, and motioned for Luke and Gridley to take a seat on the adjoining couch.

"Please, gentlemen. Make yourselves comfortable," he said as he swept his hand in the direction of the table, indicating the coffee carafe and cups spread out for them.

"Can I interest you in some piñon coffee? My wife set this out before she headed to the club for a round of golf."

"Coffee would be great," Luke replied.

"Please," Gridley added.

Eldredge set out three cups, carefully filling each with the fragrant, steaming brew as he began to speak.

"She's playing a round of golf today, if you can imagine. Not for me. Not for me."

He slid the cups over to the them and watched as they each took a sip.

"Delicious," Gridley said. "Thank you."

Luke nodded his approval as Eldredge continued.

"She's quite a woman, my wife," Eldredge continued. Then he leaned back and took a long sip of his coffee.

"Speaking of women," Gridley began, "we had a run-in with your neighbor down the road a ways."

"Beaula?" He laughed. "She's a mean old buzzard, ain't she?"

Luke nodded quickly. "She took a couple pot

shots at us when we turned down her driveway."

"That doesn't surprise me one bit. If that woman could think, she'd be dangerous."

"She seemed pretty dangerous to me!" Gridley said.

The older man laughed again. "She's always firing that gun off at strangers. I've nearly taken some buckshot myself over the years."

"She's a lunatic." Gridley exclaimed.

"Nah. We don't pay her much mind."

Gridley still looked quite concerned as the older man turned to the business at hand.

"Now then," he said, fixing his gaze on Luke. "You wanted to talk to me about Jake Dupuis."

"Yes sir, we did." Luke leaned forward. "We were wondering what you could tell us about his construction business. Particularly in relation to the inquiry you were heading up twenty years ago."

"Boy, that was sure a mess," the old man said.

He leaned back in his chair, gathering his thoughts before he spoke.

"Was Harvey Pouch involved in that in any way?" Gridley asked.

"Pouch? God yes. Those two were as thick as thieves. All of them were. Pouch, Dupuis, the good mayor. Everyone up there at city hall was up to something. Had their hands in every cookie jar."

"What exactly were you looking into, sir?" Luke

asked. "Could you give us some specifics?"

"There were a bunch of things really. My first concern was their billing. Four States Construction."

"Did Dupuis and Pouch own that?"

Eldredge nodded. "Yeah. That's what it was called back then, before Dupuis bought him out. I always wondered how that went down, Dupuis taking over, but that's a whole other topic I'm sure." He laughed again. "You wouldn't *believe* what the two of them snuck past the city. I mean *exorbitant* fees. And, no one ever questioned any of it. Well, no one but me I guess..."

"Can you give me some examples?" Luke prodded.

"Well, the one that always stands out in my mind is the Esmond Street Bridge. That thing must have taken them seven or eight years to complete. I mean, they *milked* that job for all they could. Then, when they sent the city their final bill, the amount of concrete they claimed to have used was enough for an eight-story office building, not a one-lane auto bridge. Everything was marked-up tenfold. 'Course, when I tried to bring that to the public's attention I got shut down real quick."

"Why was that?" Gridley asked.

"Simple. Conflict of interest. Dupuis was buddies with half the city council! They'd all known each other since high school. He had played ball with half of them. And pretty much all of them had a stake in his business, either on the books or under the table. There was never any question which company would be getting the really *big* contracts when they were announced."

Luke leaned forward, resting his elbows on his knees. "Was there a lot of construction money going out?"

"During the boom? *Millions.* And Four States got the bulk of it. Then of course, whenever they lost a bid by some miracle, the winning company always had nothing but fiascos. Scaffolding would fall apart, supports would collapse during construction. If it wasn't a Dupuis job, it was a disaster, and the city would inevitably bring Jake and his boys in to finish things off. For *twice* the original amount, mind you."

"So they sabotaged other jobs?" Gridley asked.

"No question!"

"If you don't mind my asking, why didn't you complete your investigation?"

"I *tried!* But you have no idea how difficult it was to get anything rolling back then. Hell, nothing has changed today I'm sure! No one wants to rock the boat..." He paused, leaning back in his chair and sighing. "Just remembering those days is exhausting. Once I started hammering away at it, I knew I hadn't even cracked the surface. There was a hell of a lot more going on than met the eye. If I'd gone any further, I was half afraid of what I'd have found. Or what they might do to keep it going."

"I'm not sure I follow you," Gridley said.

"Maybe I'm not entirely sure what I mean."

Luke watched the old man closely.

He seemed to be growing increasingly uncomfortable. Nervous even.

"Mr. Eldredge, if this is too difficult for you, we can always continue another time."

"No. I'm fine. I thought enough time had gone by that I wouldn't let that old crowd intimidate me, but it's true that old saying: The more things change, the more they stay the same." He stopped to take a sip of his coffee, wiping at his mouth with a handkerchief before he resumed. "I started to learn things I didn't really want to know. I was all for the public good, but by that point I had a family to look out for. We were starting to get hang-up calls. There was an incident with my wife's car, where she came out to the Safeway parking lot and found all the tires deflated. That sort of thing. It was getting just a little too creepy, so I stopped digging before I got too deep. All I can tell you is that this city and its government were rotten to the core. Serious corruption, and it went straight to the top. I doubt all that much has changed."

"What happened when you ended the investigation?" Luke asked.

"It all stopped. The intimidation, I mean. You know,

they all tried to play it legit. A few of them dropped off the radar for a time. But I knew whatever they had going was still moving along."

"Did you read about Harvey Pouch in the paper?" Gridley asked.

He nodded. "I did."

"Do you have any idea why he might have been killed? Who might have wanted him dead?"

Eldredge wiped at his mouth again, but didn't answer. Luke was beginning to realize this was the old man's tell, the clearest sign he was getting nervous.

"Could it have anything to do with what you've told us?" Gridley added.

"It has everything to do with it." Eldredge looked from one of them to the other. "Everything."

Gridley pulled his chair closer. "But *what* is the connection exactly? *Anything* you could tell us would be helpful."

"I've told you everything I can. Anything more and they'll know who talked."

"That's the question," Luke said. "They... Who are *they?*"

The old man struggled to his feet, dabbing at his forehead now. "I think you'd better go."

"Sir, all we need is *one* name." Gridley said.

"I've told you, you just need to look at the pieces."

He was marching to the front door now, leading them through the house.

For an old guy, he sure could move.

"I've *told* you," Eldredge said again as he pulled the door open.

"But you haven't, sir. Not clearly."

"Every name you need to know has been written up right in your own paper. Look at the names. If you want the truth, if you *really* want to know what was happening back then, and what it has to do with the dead guy in that restaurant the other night, just look to the top." He ushered them out to the front porch. "There's always been one clear winner in Farmington. *That's* where you need to look."

Luke turned to ask one more question, only to find the older gentleman quietly closing the door in his face.

Luke looked at Gridley, shrugging his shoulders as they heard the door lock behind them. "At least he didn't pull a shotgun on us, right?"

~

Gridley sat in a metal folding chair to the right of Luke's desk at The Times.

"What did you get out of that interview?" Luke asked him.

"I've interviewed a lot of witnesses over the years," Gridley said. "But I've never seen someone fall apart quite so fast."

"He seemed eager to talk at first, but something sure scared the hell out of him once he started."

"I think I might try to talk to Dupuis," Gridley said. "See if he can shed some light on things."

Red Sanders stepped out of his office at the end of the aisle. When he saw Luke and Gridley talking, a shadow passed across his face.

"Mr. Murphy, can I have a word with you please?" Red called down.

"Mr. Murphy?" Luke muttered to his guest. "This can't be good."

Gridley got to his feet. "Listen, thanks for your help."

"Thank *you*," Luke replied, as he too got to his feet. "You find anything out, keep me posted."

"Will do." Gridley nodded and walked away as Luke's editor marched up behind him.

"Who's that?" Red demanded.

"That's Detective Gridley. He's investigating the Pouch murder."

"And why is he talking to you?"

"He's keeping me appraised of updates, so I can cover any breaks in the case."

"Is *that* what you were working on all morning?" Red asked.

"Yeah. Why?"

"Pat Gleiberman has been calling here, wondering where the hell you were? You were supposed to interview that kid of his at ten o'clock this morning."

"Who?" Luke asked, looking confused. "The one with the hair? I forgot all about it. I figured this was the top priority-"

"You did, did you?" Red interrupted. "Are you the Editor-in-Chief now? Listen to me, drop this stuff with Pouch. As far as I'm concerned, some gal's jealous husband probably killed him for playing Don Juan. Case closed."

"Red, with all due respect, have you *seen* a recent photo of Harvey Pouch? He doesn't strike me as the Don Juan type-"

"Just stop playing junior detective! That story is a non-starter!" Red shouted. "Get over to the Gleiberman house now!"

"You're *serious?*" Luke couldn't tell if he was joking. "This isn't a story about some kid who won't cut his hair for the baseball team. At the bare minimum, this is about a *murder!*"

"I said drop the Pouch story. Leave it alone!"

"All right. All right." Luke muttered. "It's dropped."

What in the hell had brought this on?

He was starting to know how Ash Eldredge had felt all those years ago.

***

Owen Gleiberman was your run-of-the mill, 17 year-old, delinquent punk. He seemed to lack the decency to even be *interesting* in his manner of teenage rebellion. Baggy pants, a tank top, and a little rat moustache, all tucked under a head of unkempt, long hair.

Luke had to keep a handle on his reactions as he listened to the kid speak, struggling to keep his lip from curling or his eyes from wandering away in boredom.

"Look man, this is just bullshit," Gleiberman bemoaned. "It's like this coach, he's just a control freak. I don't know what his problem is. He's always sorta picked me outta the crowd to like browbeat and shit. This school sucks anyways. Why do I want to play baseball for them? You know?"

Luke tapped his pen on the corner of his notebook. Aside from a list of names – Pouch, Dupuis, Eldredge, and Gerritt – the bulk of the page was blank. He certainly wasn't transcribing this kid's litany of complaints.

Maybe he'd give Carley a call. Catch her up on what he'd found out.

Of course, what he'd found out wasn't much of anything, but if he was reading her signals right, it was a safe bet she hadn't put him in touch with Eldredge purely for the sake of the story. Chances were good she'd been looking for an excuse for the two of them to get together again, just as he was looking for one now.

Luke nodded his head for the zillionth time since he'd walked in the door of the Gleiberman house. Yes, that's what he'd do. He'd give her a call and see if she was interested in grabbing a bite to eat.

~

Back in high school, the unique living arrangements at the Parker house had been a teenage boy's dream come true. Assuming his girlfriend was of the same mindset. While Carley's parents lived in the two-bedroom bungalow at the front of the property, once she got to high school, they'd allowed her to move into the mother-in-law apartment around back. It was a tiny studio unit, with a kitchen and living area in the front, and the bathroom in the back. The perfect arrangement for the many nights Luke had snuck in after dark.

All these years later, as he walked around the side of the house and cut across that familiar old stretch of lawn, it also allowed Luke to knock on Carley's door, while avoiding the uncomfortable scenario of playing catch-up with her old man.

Not that he didn't like Mr. Parker. He was a perfectly nice guy, but even in his thirties, Luke would always see him as the father of the girl he was sneaking around with well after her curfew.

Luke stood on the front step, took a breath, and rapped his knuckles on the door.

It opened a crack, and Carley peeked out. Her hair was wet and wrapped in a twist of towel. She was clad in a giant terrycloth robe.

"Luke, come in. I'm was just coming back from a run when you called. I had to jump in the shower."

She led him into the studio, which had not changed a bit since their high school days. It just seemed... smaller.

"Not a problem in the least," Luke replied as he followed her inside, doing his best to avert his gaze as she slipped around the corner and out of sight.

Carley continued speaking to him from the bathroom.

"I'll just be a few minutes."

"Take your time," Luke said as he looked at a row of framed pictures of her parents. Her mother's face smiled back at him from one of the frames. She looked the same as the last time he'd seen her. Just a littler thinner. A bit gray.

Time flew.

How had so many years gone by, and how could they now feel like just the blink of an eye?

"This has been a crazy week," Carley said from the far corner of the apartment. "All of our computers have been crashing, Dorothy may be leaving to have a baby, and Dad's been needing rides to the doctor. I thought a run might help me relax, but I cut it too close. Sorry."

"Don't worry about it."

Luke glanced around the room and strolled over to the bookshelves. He ran his index finger over the bindings as he read the titles. Then his eye fell on a framed photograph that had been pushed back behind a cluster of other pictures. His eyes darted to the back of the house to be sure Carley was still busy getting ready, then he reached over and picked up the frame. It was a picture of Carley with her arms wrapped around a man in a work jacket and hat. She was leaning in, giving him a kiss on the cheek.

Ugh.

He returned the picture to its place in the back and turned around just as she came around the corner, pulling her hair into a ponytail at the back of her head.

"You ready?" she asked.

"All set."

~

They went to a place Carley suggested. Kind of a bar and grill, emphasis on grill, which meant the specialty of the house, drink-wise, was beer. Carley ordered them two Santa Fe Pales.

"I wouldn't hazard the white Russian here," Carley

noted as Luke continued to scan the drink list. "It's probably Budweiser, Coffee Mate, and cold Maxwell House."

Luke cringed. "Beer is just fine. They've got a fairly decent selection. Sure as hell better than the Genesee I was drinking back East."

He set the beer list aside and looked up.

The drinks arrived and Carley took a sip. She set her glass down and cut to the chase.

"So, Luke. You came back here to take care of your father... but if you don't mind me asking, what's keeping you in Farmington *now?* I always got the impression you were eager to get out of this place."

Luke took a long drink of his beer.

He wasn't even sure himself.

"Honestly," he began. "I don't *know* why I'm still here. I suppose it's as good a place as any. It's nice to have at least a few people who remember me as a kid."

"Did you perhaps miss the West just a little?"

"That might be part of it, too," he admitted. "Even when I was back East, it did seem like something was missing. I guess it stays in your system somehow. What about you, why are you still here?"

"I told you, the paper."

"But you could always sell it. I'm sure your Dad would understand."

"I wouldn't get much for it. And... I suppose I

missed being back here too. It's reassuring to know there's a place you can return to when you need to regroup."

"Isn't that the truth," he agreed.

They looked at each other for a moment.

"It sounds like we were both looking for home," she observed.

"Maybe so. But you know, I actually envy you. I always have..."

You envy *me?* I can't imagine why! You're the one who's had the adventures. You at least *left the state!*"

"That's only because I didn't have much to leave here. It was just me and the old man. And he was never particularly fond of me."

"I don't think that's true," Carley said. "Your father was just... reserved."

"That's one term for it. But growing up, you and your parents always seemed so close. I loved being around that. It was comforting."

"Yeah... like I said. I guess that's why I'm still here." She seemed embarrassed and jumped to change the subject. "So anyway, what happened at Eldredge's place today?"

"Oh, wait until you hear this!" Luke said, pulling his chair closer and hunching over his drink as he settled in to recount the day's events.

Mike Attebery

5.

Luke sat at his desk, working half-heartedly to fashion an article out of what snippets he could recall from his interview with Gleiberman. Nothing was coming to mind. He was debating heading to the kitchen for another cup of burned coffee, but wary of crossing the newsroom and drawing Red's attention if the old man happened to be looking out his office window. The internal struggle of caffeine addiction versus the boss' disdain was thankfully interrupted when the phone rang.

The caller ID displayed Mick Gridley's number.

Luke hugged the phone, murmuring into the handset as he watched Red's office door.

"Yeah? What's the latest?"

~

Ten minutes later, Luke was seated in Gridley's office at police headquarters.

"I paid a visit to John Dupuis' office. No cooperation from anyone working there, either.

Big surprise, right?" Gridley said. "They told me if I wanted their help I'd have to come back with a warrant."

Luke leaned back in his seat. From this position he could see out Gridley's office door, and down the corridor to the front desk.

"I suppose you can't blame them. We don't really have reason to question him," Luke said as he arched his neck.

"No *official* reason, but their reaction still makes me damn suspicious."

The front doors swung open. From the corner of his eye, Luke noticed a familiar individual entering the lobby, headed for the front desk. It was the old guy in the purple baseball cap and overalls, who had been speaking to Grace a few days ago. Luke strained to hear what he was saying.

"What do I have to do to get you people out there to see for yourselves?" the old man pleaded.

The uniformed officer at the front desk was trying to assuage his concerns, just as Grace had. "Sir, I've told you, there's nothing we can do about noises in the canyon, it's outside-"

Gridley noticed Luke's distraction. "What's going on?"

Luke nodded toward the commotion. "I see you guys get the same bunch of characters we do."

"My wife is sick!" The old man shouted. "These

trucks don't let her get any sleep!"

"You get that guy too? He keeps coming in complaining about trucks or something." Gridley walked over and shut his office door. "You know how it is. Libraries, police stations, and newspapers, they keep the crazies occupied."

Luke returned his attention to their conversation. "Let's just hope that by the time you *do* find a way to get a warrant, Dupuis' files haven't gone up in flames like Pouch's place."

"Don't think I haven't thought that," Gridley mused.

"You know, I might go down and look through the town records. See what I can find out about that property Pouch owned. It could just be the way my friend's father discussed it, but I can't help but think there's a connection."

~

The records office was a huge, high-ceilinged building, with aisle upon aisle of filing cabinets and ladders on wheels. Ceiling fans rotated lazily overhead, casting spinning, stretching shadows around the room. Somehow, the city had never managed to convert all this old paperwork over to digital files. Now, Luke couldn't help but wonder if that had been a conscious decision by the folks in power. As long as the interested parties had to haul their asses down here to dig through the documents themselves, they were probably a hell of a lot less likely to do it. And, as an added bonus, the people working here could report back on anyone who stopped in, looking at paperwork.

And they could get a look at your face.

Luke had been relieved to walk in the door and recognize the guy working the front desk. In his mid-to-late 70s, Charlie Moss struck Luke as the quintessential small-town old timer. He'd also been a friend of his father's, a fact that reassured him that, at least on this watch, his visit to the records hall wouldn't be reported back to anyone connected to Dupuis or Gerritt.

Luke was standing atop one of the ladders, searching through the topmost drawer of a massive wooden file cabinet. Whoever had designed this place must have nourished a gothically perverse sense of humor. He wasn't having any luck. Luke slammed the drawer shut and climbed down the creaky ladder.

Charlie straightened his heavy glasses, squinting up at him with a pleasant smile. "Anything I can help you with, Luke?"

Luke leaned against the ladder, debating how much he should risk saying.

The hell with it, if he couldn't trust one of his old man's friends, who in the hell could he trust in this town. Right?

"Yeah, Charlie," Luke said in a soft voice. He

looked around the hall to make sure they were the only two people there. "I've been trying to get a little history on a piece of land Harvey Pouch used to own. But I'm not having any luck."

"You mean the property where they're building the new arena." Charlie said. "What do you want to know?"

"I don't even know exactly. I've just heard there's some controversy connected with the way it's changed hands over the years. I'm curious to see who's owned it and what Pouch and his former father-in-law might have seen in it."

"You mean Mayor Gerritt."

"Yeah, old Ben."

"That always used to be city property. Had been since I was a boy," Charlie said. "Right up until Gerritt took office and quietly pushed the sale through to his daughter's fiancé. The city passed it off as a way to raise revenues from worthless land, but everyone knew Gerritt was behind that."

"What did Pouch want with it?"

"Beats me. As far back as I can remember, the only thing on that land was a couple of rusted pumpjacks. As far as controversy goes, I don't recall anybody really saying 'boo' about it. Maybe a few arched eyebrows around city hall, but it was just one of those things. Rich guys helping their relatives buy stuff they'll probably never use."

"But if ramping up city revenue was the goal, it doesn't sound like Harvey paid much for it."

"If I recall correctly, your father thought that was odd too," Charlie noted. "Of course, Mike Murphy was always on guard where Ben Gerritt was concerned."

"What did you think, Charlie?"

Charlie brought a hand to his chin, pondering his answer.

"Your father was probably on the right track. Let me put it this way, why else would a guy like Ben Gerritt, worth plenty of money, free to do whatever he damn well pleases, *ever* want to be mayor of a city like this in the first place?"

Luke shrugged. "To give back to the community?"

Charlie fixed him with a narrow gaze. "Please. I've got no illusions about it. To add to his bottom line. The only reason folks like Gerritt stay in places like Farmington is because they've figured out how to work the system from the inside. It's worth their while to stick around, work with what they know, and what they can control, to make as much money for themselves and their relatives as they possibly can."

"Charlie, I never took you for such a cynic."

"Trust me. When you get to be my age, you've seen it all. Gerritt had the land sold to Harvey Pouch. Pouch sold it back to the city at a loss. Years later, the city practically *gave* a chunk of it to Gerritt for his arena. There might have been a few hiccups in the plan, what with Harvey going bankrupt and Melanie getting a divorce, but I'm sure it's nothing Ben Gerritt didn't anticipate."

"But you have no theories?"

Charlie shrugged.

"Watchdogging Ben Gerritt was your father's hobby. Not mine. What's a city clerk like me stand to gain by nursing theories on the shenanigans these people do?"

"You think there are any files on it in here?"

"I haven't seen anything, and if I ain't seen it, I doubt anyone else has. You could always chat with some of the folks at city hall, see if anyone there remembers something, but I can't think of anything that's down on paper."

Luke looked at his watch. He could probably get over there before the end of the day, but it felt like he was grasping at straws.

Ah, what the hell...

"Thanks Charlie," he said as he headed for the door. "I think I might do that."

~

Luke waited for the receptionist at the front counter to get off the phone.

It was near the end of the work day, which meant everyone who was anyone at city hall had cleared out hours ago. Some of them had probably walked across the parking lot to the Elks Lodge for a drink. The rest were likely working the angles at bars all over town. The look of the city offices screamed *70s*, which meant the last time the city had redone the mayor's offices, Ben Gerritt had been the man in charge.

Luke waited for the woman to wrap up her call. It certainly didn't sound like it was work-related. The nameplate on her desk read Amber Smith. Judging from Amber's appearance, she was in her mid-50s. Another woman was typing at a computer behind a cubicle wall in the corner. Luke couldn't get a clear look at her, but if he had to guess, he'd have said she was in her early 60s. That put her just *barely* in the range of Gerritt's years in office.

Luke was debating whether or not he should just walk around the desk and speak to the other woman, when Amber finally hung up the phone.

"Can I help you sir?"

"Yes, I'm from *The Daily Times*. I'm working on a piece about Ben Gerritt and the history of the arena project. It's sort of a retrospective on his years of service for the city, and I'm wondering if anyone in the building might have worked here in the years Gerritt was mayor."

Luke heard the typing behind the cubicle wall stop.

He caught Amber's eyes dart to the side for a split-second.

"Umm, I'm not sure. Did you have a specific question for them?" she asked.

"I'm just looking for some anecdotes, maybe answer a few questions about the property and how long Gerritt has been fighting to get the arena built for Farmington."

Amber cleared her throat.

"No, I'm afraid everyone who worked in the offices for Gerritt's administration has been retired for quite a while."

"That's too bad," Luke said. "Are you certain about that?

"I'm afraid so."

He pulled a business card from his pocket and set it on the counter.

"Well, I'll just leave my number with you to be safe. If you happen to think of anyone, please ask them to give me a call."

***

Detective Gridley pulled his car up to a pair of towering iron gates at the entrance to the large estate. *GERRITT* was emblazoned across the arch that loomed overhead.

Mick had decided there was no harm in getting a little daring with his random drop-ins. After all, what did a retired mayor have to fear in answering questions about his deceased former son-in-law? Nothing, if he was on the up and up. It was just a detective stopping by in the process of conducting a thorough investigation into a seemingly random tragedy.

Gridley leaned out the driver's side window and pushed a button on the intercom panel to the side of the driveway. A moment later, a woman's tinny voice crackled from the speaker:

"May I help you?"

"Yes, this is Detective Gridley with the Farmington Police Department."

After a beat...

"Can I ask what this is in reference to?"

"I just have some routine questions for Mr. Gerritt.

"Questions concerning-?"

"The murder of Harvey Pouch."

There was another long pause.

Then a chime sounded, and the gates parted before him.

"Please park at the office bungalow."

Gridley pulled through the gates and drove down a long, winding dirt road. He crossed over a small stream, and past several fields of cattle, until he came to a sign directing him to the estate's main office. Gridley parked in front of a complex of small, interconnected buildings and got out of his car.

This was one hell of an operation Gerritt was running out here. Philanthropy was clearly not the old man's only game.

Gridley headed into the nearest building. He emerged in an elaborately decorated lobby. An artificial waterfall splashed quietly to the side of a seating area, where a young woman in her late-20s greeted him.

"Detective Gridley?"

"Yes."

"I'm afraid Mr. Gerritt is in meetings for the remainder of the day."

"Oh, I'm a little confused. The woman I spoke to at the front gate said to drive through."

"Yes, I know. That was me."

Gridley narrowed his eyes, trying to puzzle out what was going on here. "Why did you ask me to come down here then?

"I'm sorry for the inconvenience. This is a rather busy time at the moment. Do you have a card? We'd be more than happy to get back to you to schedule a meeting with Mr. Gerritt."

"Umm, yeah, sure.

Gridley handed the woman one of his cards, which she accepted without even looking at it.

"Thank you, Detective."

Gridley waited for her to say something more, but

that appeared to be it. With a nod of her head, she spun on her heel and walked away, leaving Gridley standing alone. The artificial waterfall splashed soothingly to his side.

"OK, then. I'll just... see myself out," he muttered to himself.

He walked out of the building slowly, half-expecting someone to come running after him at the last moment, eager to know what a police detective was doing in the lobby, but when no one stopped him, he climbed into his car and drove back the way he had come.

Moments after he drove back through the front gates, a car with dark, tinted windows pulled out of Gerritt's driveway, and followed after him.

6.

Carley stood at the counter in her tiny kitchen, slicing up ingredients. She was fixing dinner as Luke filled her in on the day's events.

"How do you and Gridley think the land ties into Harvey Pouch's murder?" she asked.

"We don't know. But when we asked Ash Eldredge about his investigation, he started talking about all these questionable construction bids and work assignments between the city and Dupuis' folks. All of them occurring while Gerritt was mayor.

"And the land, these jobs, all of this stuff from decades ago, somehow ties back to Harvey Pouch getting his throat slashed over a plate of enchiladas last week?"

"Fajitas," Luke corrected, which prompted Carley to mimic stabbing him as well. "As he put it, Harvey Pouch's murder and all the corruption back then had 'everything' to do with what's happened this week. Aside from Dupuis and Harvey's business, the only thing I can figure the three of them – Dupuis,

Pouch, and Gerritt – had in common was that land. Everything else was Pouch and Dupuis or Pouch and Gerritt. With the arena, Harvey is the conduit between the two men with the strongest connection to that property right here and now."

"But what about *that* is so unique?"

"Nothing that I can think of. Like Charlie Moss said, the only thing on that land before the arena was a couple of broken down pumpjacks."

"And Pouch had no involvement in the arena?"

"None."

Carley poured herself a glass of wine and looked over at the TV, where Ben Gerritt suddenly appeared on the screen.

"Well speak of the devil," she said. "Look who it is."

She grabbed the remote and turned up the volume.

A reporter was speaking over footage of the former mayor shaking hands at an event.

"Rumors are growing about a possible run for governor by Ben Gerritt. Gerritt, who is heading into the home stretch on an ambitious and long-running sports and entertainment facility outside Farmington, has reemerged on the public scene recently, and that has political junkies in New Mexico talking. Gerritt's office has yet to respond to the rumors."

"Guess someone else has our theory," Luke

replied.

"I'll bet he runs."

"I'm *sure* he will-"

Luke was interrupted by the ringing of his cellphone. He answered the call the moment he saw Gridley's name on the display.

"Hey, what's happening?"

He set his beer down with a *thunk*.

"Let me give you an address."

~

Gridley sat at Carley's kitchen counter with a bag of ice held to his swollen eye. His face was bruised. His shirt was torn down the front.

"Hell of a way to make your introduction," he muttered to Carley.

"Hell of a way to treat a police officer," she said. "Let me see how it's doing."

Carley snuck a peek at Gridley's eye as he pulled the ice pack away. The upper lid had practically swelled shut.

"Jesus!" Luke exclaimed, recoiling at the sight of it. "They really worked you over! What the hell happened?"

"I caught sight of a car following me almost the moment I left Ben Gerritt's place this afternoon. I did my best to lose them, but they showed up outside headquarters as I was leaving tonight. Three guys.

They jumped me. Told me I needed to stop asking so many questions about Ben Gerritt. That I was starting to irritate people."

"Any idea who they were?" Luke asked.

"Nope. Two guys in baseball caps, they stayed in the back. Third guy had dark eyes, a thick moustache, and a cowboy hat, he's the one who gave me the warning. He roughed me up while the other two beat the shit out of my car."

"And this was outside headquarters?!" Carley said. "No one came out to stop it?"

Gridley shook his head. "Not a one, and it would have been impossible to miss it."

"Did you report it?"

"Nope. And I'm not going to. As he was leaving, the guy with the moustache made a special point of telling me folks in the department would be distinctly unsympathetic if I reported what had happened. Not that I had planned to anyway."

"What do you mean?" Carley asked.

"We're finding people in the department aren't exactly welcoming Mick with open arms," Luke explained.

"There is one upside to this," Gridley said. "The fact that it happened *right* after I tried to talk with Gerritt tells me I'm getting under the skin of the right people."

"Or the very *wrong* ones," Luke said. "I guess

we can state with some confidence now that they definitely have people inside the department."

"Sure as hell seems that way."

The room grew quiet as they considered just what that realization meant.

"Okay, so let's see where things stand," Gridley said, breaking the silence. "We have Harvey Pouch murdered, his house and office torched. A former business associate who won't talk to the media or the police."

Luke continued. "We have an old timer too afraid to talk, but who thinks Pouch's murder had something to do with land he sold to the city. Property the city then broke up and sold piecemeal to its former mayor, a man who is now building a sports arena on that very piece of land, *with* the dead man's former business partner!"

"*And* we have a butt-load of buildings out there in the canyon, which, according to your witness, owe their very existence to unheard of corruption in the city government," Carley said. "And on top of all *that,* Ben Gerritt looks like he may be a candidate for governor."

"A candidate who most-likely had a police detective attacked when he started asking too many questions," Gridley concluded.

Carley sipped her wine. "Did you want any of this?" she asked Gridley as she held up the bottle.

"I better not."

"Suit yourself," she said, refilling her own glass as she continued to think aloud. "Are we looking at the fallout from some long-standing business disagreement?"

"I don't think we have enough information," Luke said. "We're missing some key piece of the puzzle."

"I'm too tired to think about it anymore tonight," Gridley sighed. "I'm gonna head home and get some sleep. This whole mess can wait until tomorrow."

"So you're *not* gonna drop it?" Luke asked.

"*Of course not*. They just pissed me off!" He flashed a bloody smile. "Now I *really* want to know what's going on."

Gridley headed for the door. "Carley, it was a pleasure meeting you."

"Same here, Detective."

"Mick," he said, before turning to Luke and giving him a wink. "I'll see you tomorrow."

"See you tomorrow," Luke said as he closed the door behind him.

"This whole situation makes me nervous," Carley said.

"You and me both."

"As a journalist, I love the story, but as a pragmatist, I almost wish you'd drop it and cover the stories Red assigns you."

"You'd rather I wrote about high school athletes who

refuse to cut their hair?"

"I just can't help but wonder what will happen when this starts to get out."

~

Gridley walked across the back yard and around the side of the main house to the street. The neighborhood was silent. Most of the front lights on the few houses that dotted the block were now extinguished. The only light came from a single street light at the corner.

Gridley picked up the pace as he headed down the block, finding the sounds of his own footsteps oddly unsettling. He had just passed a row of hedges, and was about thirty feet from his car, when he heard another set of footsteps join the echoes of his own.

Then he heard *more* sets of feet join the others. *Shit.*

He picked up the pace as he stole a look over his shoulder. Three men in cowboy hats had stepped out from the bushes and were following him. The guy with the moustache, who'd headed up the first attack, was once more in the lead.

Gridley took off running as he dug into his pockets for his keys. He made it to the car, and was fumbling with the lock, when a hand grabbed his shoulder and spun him around. The guy with the moustache was in his face now.

"You don't listen too good, do you, asshole?"

"What?" Gridley asked with a smirk, only to be pulled forward and slammed face first onto the hood of the car.

"Didn't I tell you to keep your mouth shut?"

He looked up and saw that he was surrounded.

"What are you doing talking to a couple of *reporters?* That was a stupid move, Detective. A very stupid move."

Gridley's eyes darted from one man to the next. He looked back at their leader, who was pulling his arm back, winding up to take a swing. Just as the guy started to move, Gridley saw light flash off the revolver clasped in the palm of his hand. Before he could raise his arms in self-defense, his assailant swung around as hard as he could, smashing the gun grip into Gridley's face.

~

Luke was walking toward the *Daily Times* building, taking a swig of his morning coffee, when he caught sight of Ben Gerritt walking out of the main entrance. Luke stopped at the edge of the parking lot. He wondered if the old man had seen him. Two men in cowboy hats were walking with Gerritt, one at either side. Luke hesitated, then continued toward the building. He was ready to raise a hand in greeting, but Gerritt just looked him in the eye as he approached, then kept walking.

Probably not a good sign.

Luke strolled past Grace's front station, en route to his desk. He glanced around his workspace to see if anything had been moved.

Red Sanders stepped out of his office. The old man's expression was grim. "Luke, could I have a word with you?"

"Sure, Red," Luke answered uncertainly.

He trudged past his editor's glowering face and took a seat. Red shut the door behind them.

~

"You can use this desk. Coffee and filters are in the cabinet over the machine in the kitchen. Other than that, you should know your way around already."

Carley was standing in front of a beat-up metal desk in the middle of what passed for *The Aztec Review's* newsroom. It was basically an old, wood-paneled office, with a wall of strip-mall style windows that let light into the hopelessly outdated interior.

"Thanks, Carley."

"You're not gonna have quite as many readers as *The Times*, but we added *five* new Facebook fans last week, so you're gonna have one hell of an online presence!"

Luke cracked a smile, the first in a day that had started out quite badly.

"That was the shortest job search of my life," he said.

"And probably not your last, but I'll save our balance sheets for another time," Carley said. "For now, you're with the good guys."

Luke tossed his notebook on the desk and looked around.

"Is that all your stuff?" Carley asked.

"I don't like to keep much stuff at work."

"I suppose I can see why!"

"I shouldn't be surprised, right?" Luke asked. "Gerritt owns the damn paper, so of course he had me thrown out of the place-"

Luke was interrupted by the chime of the front door, and looked up to see a familiar face coming in the door. It was the old timer with the purple cap and the overalls!

This felt like home already!

The old guy strolled up to the front counter, where Marion, a matronly woman who helmed *The Review's* front counter, fielded his immediate stream of complaints.

"What do you suppose Gerritt will do when he finds out you're writing over here?" Carley asked.

"I haven't got the slightest idea, but don't be

surprised if a Molotov cocktail comes flying through your front windows."

Marion had to raise her voice for the old man to hear her. "Sir, there's nothing we can do about it! You need to complain to the City of Farmington."

"I *have* complained to them. I've complained to the city, the police, *and* to *The Times,* but no one will listen!!"

"Well, then I don't know what to tell you."

Luke's head spun around. This was the third time he'd crossed paths with this man. He hurried to the front desk.

"Hold it," Luke said. "Sir, tell it one more time. Tell *me* what's going on."

The old guy turned with a scowl. He looked Luke up and down slowly, then he cleared his throat and launched into it.

"I live out by the highway, just at the entrance to the canyon, if you know where that is."

Luke nodded. "That's right by my father's house. On the way to the new arena, if I'm not mistaken."

"That's right."

"Now what's this problem you're having? It's with trucks, right? The noise from trucks."

"That's right," the old guy said. "Damn near every night, just after midnight, a caravan of trucks starts rolling past my house into the canyon. They just keep on coming, moving in and out in convoys, straight through the night until just about dawn. My wife is extremely sick, and she *cannot* get a decent night's sleep with the noise."

"And these are trucks like pickup trucks?"

"No!" The old man said incredulously. "These are trucks like tractor trailer trucks, *tankers.*"

A shiver ran up Luke's spine.

"And you have no idea whose vehicles they are?"

"If I knew, I'd be at *their* office, shouting my head off! All I know is if my wife wasn't dying already, these trucks would be killing her. They *are* killing her."

Luke headed for the door, slipping on his jacket and pulling his keys from his pocket as he did so.

"Sir, tell me *exactly* where I need to go."

***

Luke drove out to the edge of Chokecherry Canyon, killing his Mustang's headlights as he circled up to the top of a mesa with a particularly clear view of the entrance to the canyon. From there, he could see right down to the expanse of land on which Gerritt's arena was taking shape. He parked his car near a cluster of gnarled trees, where it would blend into the darkness as the light in the sky grew dim. When the temperature had begun to drop, as it always did in the desert, he put up the top, pulled on a thick sweatshirt, and started in on the bag of Lotaburgers he'd brought with him from town.

He sat in the darkness, eating fast food, pondering the strange shape of Lotaburger's red straws, and peering out into the darkness through his binoculars. Now and then he scanned the area, starting on the floor of the canyon, then sweeping over to the far-off silhouette of his father's house, which he could just make out in the darkness, then over to a small, dark bungalow with one light glowing on the front porch. That was where the old man and his wife lived. Luke lowered the binoculars and sipped his chocolate shake.

This was going to be a long night.

The stars were glimmering in the crystal clear sky. Luke allowed himself to relax, feeling the tension in his shoulders unwinding as he slid the seat back and stretched out his legs. He found his thoughts turning to Carley, wondering what she was doing at that moment...

The next thing he knew, he was jolted awake, startled by a clap of thunder that reverberated in the desert air. But when he looked around, the stars were still shining, the sky was still clear. The clock radio showed it was just after midnight. Then the rumbling sound grew louder. It wasn't thunder, it was the roar of a diesel engine. Suddenly, a tanker roared past him, just as several more trucks came thundering into view behind it. Luke watched the vehicles' headlights bouncing up and down in his rear-view mirror as they came up behind him, fast. Just as quickly as he saw them, they passed him by, plowing ahead on the dirt road, then turning and plunging down the steep descent into the canyon. More trucks followed suit, until there were a half-dozen enormous tankers belching out black smoke and kicking up clouds of dust, as they roared away in the direction of the dimly lit arena. The rumble of the engines echoed back and forth against the sandstone cliffs surrounding the canyon.

No wonder that man's poor wife couldn't sleep!

Luke peered through the binoculars as the caravan raced across the canyon floor and slipped out of view; then he tossed them on the passenger seat and started the engine. He left the Mustang's headlights off as he stepped on the gas and traced the trucks' path, managing to catch up relatively quickly. He was driving just fast enough that his pulse began racing a little as he closed the gap, but not so recklessly that he might lose control of the vehicle or be seen by an alert driver.

Once the trucks reached the arena grounds, they cut their speed in half, slowing as they reached the security gates that surrounded the property. Luke held back, pulling off to the side and watching from afar as the trucks made their way through the compound of buildings, before eventually pulling through an opening in the side of the arena. They streamed into the towering structure one after another, then the massive door rumbled closed behind them.

Luke watched it all through his binoculars.

What in the hell was going on?

Mike Attebery

7.

Luke was on the phone at his new desk, sipping coffee as he waited for the person on the other end of the line to track Gridley down at police headquarters. He'd been trying to get ahold of the detective since the previous night, but call after call had gone straight to voicemail. He was starting to get worried.

"I've *tried* his cell phone," He exclaimed. "I've *tried* his work number. I can't get an answer at either of them." He brushed the hair from his forehead, doing his best to keep his temper in check. "Look, when Detective Gridley comes in can you do me a favor? Can you tell him to call Luke Murphy ASAP? Yes, he has my number. Thank you."

"Just a thought," Marion said as Luke got to his feet and paced past her desk. "Maybe he was sleeping?"

"Let's hope that's the case, but I doubt it."

The front door chimed *loudly,* and Luke and Marion turned to see Carley walking through the door. Judging from the look on her face, she had news, and it wasn't good.

"Luke, they just found your friend Gridley."

~

A crowd of police officers was scattered across the area overlooking an arroyo. Luke was slightly disoriented as he made his way through the crowd. The few that noticed his presence appeared to pay him no mind. They were used to him showing up at scenes like this, preparing stories for *The Times*.

Luke saw Sonny West and headed his way. Sonny gave him a look as Luke walked up beside him, but otherwise, he seemed unusually subdued, almost cold.

"You found Gridley?" Luke asked breathlessly.

Sonny nodded. "They're bringing him up now."

A shiver ran down Luke's back as he followed Sonny to the side of the arroyo.

"What do you mean 'bringing him up?'"

Luke caught up to Sonny and looked over his shoulder, just as several officers pulled a crumpled, bloodied body out of the sand and rolled it in a body bag they'd spread out on the ground.

It was Gridley.

The detective's beard was covered in sand. His face was splattered in blood and grime.

Luke watched as they zipped the bag shut. He

tried to force his way forward, but Sonny stepped in his way.

"What happened?!"

"It looks like he got himself into some trouble," Sonny said, putting his hand on Luke's shoulder, pushing him back on his heels. "Luke, I'm gonna have to ask you to leave."

"Why?! What the hell *happened?!*"

"You can't be here. You can't be here."

"I'm a reporter! He's a friend of mine! You can't make me leave."

Sonny sighed. "I'm afraid I can't cooperate with you."

Luke's voice dropped as the strength oozed from his limbs.

"You've always cooperated with me. What's going on?"

"What can I tell you, man? This is different."

Luke's eyes were starting to sting. He could feel the corners of his mouth pulling down.

"This is a very different situation," Sonny continued. "I wouldn't get any more involved if I were you."

Several uniformed officers had turned up now. They stood off to the sides, watching Luke and Sonny closely. When Luke again tried to approach the edge of the hillside, two of the officers stepped in, one on each side of Sonny.

"Go home and forget about it, Luke. Go home and

forget about it."

~

Luke tried to reach Carley, but he wasn't getting any answer.

He held the phone, rubbing his temples as he watched the muted TV across the room. Footage of Gridley's bagged body being removed from the scene filled the broadcast. Luke ended the call, and practically jumped out of his skin when his phone immediately began ringing.

"Carley?!"

A woman's voice came on the line. Someone he didn't know. "Mr. Murphy?"

"Yes?"

"Luke Murphy?"

"That's correct. Who is this?"

"I thought you might want to meet with me."

"Who is this?" Luke was growing wary.

"You left your card at the front desk the other day. My name is Faye Burkhardt. I worked at city hall when Ben Gerritt was the mayor... I guess you'd say I was his mistress."

Luke sat bolt upright.

"Where would you like to meet?"

~

Faye Burkhardt was showing her age, which appeared to be her early 60s, but it was obvious she had been a knockout in her younger days. Hell, she was *still* an attractive woman. She was also very nervous talking to Luke. She sat calmly, and she spoke clearly, but the way she was sucking down cigarettes betrayed her nerves. She tapped ashes into an ashtray that sat in the middle of the coffee table in her living room. Much like the mayor's office, the place looked like it had been decorated in the 70s and left untouched ever since.

"I'm not entirely sure why I'm talking to you. You just had an honest voice when you came to city hall, so I thought 'What the hell?' maybe I can trust him..." She exhaled a cloud of smoke. "Besides, I think its time *someone* said something."

Luke took a miniature recorder from his pocket. "Do you mind if I record this?"

Faye shook her head. "Go ahead."

Luke pressed RECORD and set the recorder on the table.

"Can you tell me how long you were involved with Ben Gerritt?"

"Two years, while his wife was alive, and close to three years after the accident."

"Which accident do you mean?"

"The plane crash, when Mrs. Gerritt was killed."

Luke nodded.

"And you were his secretary during this time as well?"

"How do you think we met?"

"Between the two positions, you probably got a good idea of everything that went on."

"Two positions?" She laughed and took a drag on her cigarette. "Give an old girl some credit."

Luke looked at her blankly.

"That was a joke," Faye said as she exhaled a cloud of smoke. "But yeah, I had a pretty good idea of everything he had going on."

"Do you know anything about Harvey Pouch?"

"What do you want to know?"

"Did Gerritt like him?"

"He did, for the first year or so that Pouch was married to Melanie. Thought of him like the son he never had. But that changed later on."

"What happened?"

"Oh, a few things. The marriage didn't work out. Pouch dropped out of a few deals. But mostly I think Ben just went sour on him. He does that with people, one minute you're on his good side, the next he has no use for you, so he wants nothing to do with you."

"Did it have anything to do with the property Pouch bought from the town?"

"Undoubtedly," she said without missing a beat.

"Do you think that land had anything to do with Harvey Pouch's death."

"I'm *sure* it did."

Luke paused, waiting for her to elaborate.

"Ben wanted that for himself. He wanted it *bad*. But there was no way for him to get his hands on it while he was mayor. I mean, old Ben could get away with a lot, but even *he'd* get called out on a deal *that* cozy."

"Why'd he want it so badly?"

"That's something I don't know," she said. "But the next best thing to getting it for himself was to keep it in the family, so that's what he did, made it so Harvey Pouch could snatch it up instead. People still raised some eyebrows, but like most things, Ben got away with it."

"And is that the business deal Harvey backed out of?"

"One of them."

"Do you know how Pouch lost his money?"

Faye laughed. "That's the beauty of it. Turned out he never had that much to begin with, but somehow Ben and Melanie were convinced he truly was big-time. You think that little tramp would have married him if she'd known he wasn't loaded? And old Ben would never have pushed so hard for Melanie to get with him if he'd known the truth."

"So then, how did he lose what he had?"

"Gambling. Drinking. Harvey was always taking off in the middle of the night for Vegas. He'd either bet everything he owned, or sell it, and bet the money."

"Everything but the land, right?"

"Everything but the land. And believe me, Ben tried to buy it from him a million times."

"Did Gerritt ever threaten him?"

"I wouldn't doubt it. That man has a lot of layers. Some of them can be pretty harsh." She laughed. "Like those damn drinks he's so fond of..."

Luke nodded, picturing the unmixed cocktail Gerritt had downed at the country club.

"He *seems* sweet," Faye continued. "But he'll knock you on your ass if you don't watch yourself. He's always got something extra going on, and if you cross him, there's some definite anger there, just below the surface."

"What's he have to be angry about?"

Faye shrugged. "Someone having something he doesn't? Unless of course the other guy is Jake Dupuis. Those two were into everything together, even back then. But yeah, as far as Ben is concerned, he'll do whatever it takes to beat the other guy."

"Would he kill?"

"I'm not sure Ben could kill a man *himself.*"

"But you think he'd have someone killed?

Faye took another deep drag from her cigarette. "Oh yeah. In a heartbeat."

~

Luke was listening to the interview as he drove back from Faye Burkhardt's place. He was just reaching over to turn up the volume on the recorder when a pair of headlights appeared in his rearview mirror, causing the hairs on the back of his neck to stand on end. He stopped the tape, gripped the wheel tightly, and stepped on the gas.

But the headlights kept getting closer.

Whoever was driving the approaching car was closing the distance between them. *Fast.*

Luke's eyes darted to the rearview mirror, then back to the road as he continued to accelerate.

A hulking pickup truck emerged from the darkness behind him, its grill glimmering like clenched teeth as it raced over the roadway. The noise of its engine grew increasingly louder, until it was *roaring* toward Luke's old Mustang, gobbling up asphalt as it closed the gap.

Someone was pushing that beaten-up truck for all it was worth.

Luke dropped a gear and stomped on the gas as his pursuer continued to gain on him. It was impossible to make out the face of the driver or determine whether there was anyone else in the truck. The roadway bent slightly, til it was running parallel to the river.

The truck was *really* hauling ass now as it veered into the next lane and pulled up alongside him. That's when the *real* fun began. Without warning, the driver swerved the truck to the side, forcing Luke onto the gravel on the edge of the road. He managed to avoid the truck's first two attacks, but on the third attempt, the vehicles collided, driving the Mustang to the side as Luke struggled to maintain control of the vehicle.

He stomped on the gas again, but the truck's driver followed suit. Finally, as the two cars raced side by side, Luke slammed on the brakes, downshifting as he did so. Smoke belched from his tires as the truck shot ahead of him. Luke cranked the steering wheel, somehow managing to get the car turned around in the opposite direction as the truck's tires squealed to a stop further up the road.

He glanced in the rearview mirror and saw the truck's headlights as it turned around and started back in his direction. Luke was trying desperately to get his old car back up to speed, but his pursuer was gaining ground again at an unnerving rate. Before Luke knew what was happening, the other vehicle had once more pulled up alongside him. Then it swerved back into his lane.

Luke jerked the wheel to the side and fought to stay in control. He looked up and saw the headlights of an oncoming car quickly approaching in the truck's lane. The truck swerved toward Luke one last time, gunning its engine and pulling in front of him, just as the other car passed by.

This guy was insane!

Without warning, the truck's driver slammed on the brakes. Luke shouted as he swerved out of the way. The next thing he knew, he was plowing through the brush on the side of the road, barreling down the embankment as the river appeared before him. The Mustang plunged into the river. Luke hit the water with a jolt as he and the car were pulled along by the current.

Silence swept in as water enveloped the Mustang. Luke looked up the embankment and saw the truck slow down for a moment, then race away, its tires squealing. The river was moving quickly, but Luke managed to climb out the driver's-side window and make his way to the edge of the river. He pulled himself up on shore, and collapsed on the mud in exhaustion.

Mike Attebery

8.

The Mustang looked pathetic sitting in front of Nick's Auto Repair, water trickling from every pipe, gasket, and hose. Luke couldn't imagine where it could still be *coming from* after this much time had gone by. It had been at least two hours since the car had been hauled out of the river and towed into town. He sat in a folding chair in front of the shop, listening to Nick talking on the phone, calling up each of his buddies, one by one, and telling them what a sorry mess he had sitting at his shop right now.

Luke half-wondered if Nick was referring to the car or to *him*.

He was admittedly rattled by what had just happened.

Nick was a heavy-set mechanic who had done a bit of work on Luke's car from time to time since he'd returned to the area, just enough to keep the thing running, but never anything more. Other than cosmetic concerns and a few oil changes, there had never been much the old car *needed* to have done. Now, as Nick paced around the soggy old convertible, opening doors and throwing up his arms in amazement as more water continued to pour out, Luke could practically *see* the dollar signs floating through the mechanic's head. This car was gonna be the source of some very nice income for the foreseeable future.

Nick hung up his phone. He circled the car one last time. Stopped. Pulled a cigar from his breast pocket, and popped it in his mouth.

"Well, now this is a first for me." He bit off the end of the cigar and spit it on the ground. "Yep, this is gonna cost you some money."

"That's fine," Luke said. "Just as long as you can save it."

"Oh sure, we can save her. I can fix her up *real* nice. It's just gonna take some time." He lit the cigar and took a long drag. "And it's gonna cost you some dough."

Luke sighed. "Do you have something I can drive until then?"

Nick paused to exhale a massive cloud of smoke.

"Yeah, I got somethin' you can use. Guy skipped out on his repair bill last spring, left me to figure out what in the hell to do with it. I'm just looking for someone to cover the cost of repairs and get the thing out of here."

"Great, where is it?"

'Round back," Nick replied as he led Luke around the side of the building.

The yard in back of the garage was illuminated by a couple of large security lights, which cast the lot in a harsh yellow cloud.

"That's it," Nick said as he pointed at a rusty food truck in the shape of a gigantic, hard-shell taco. "Guy owned The Taco Platter out on 20th."

Luke stared at the car dumbly.

"It's a Mexican joint," Nick added.

"I can see that. Is that the only thing you have?"

"That's it."

Nick dug a set of keys out of his pocket and dangled them in front of Luke's face. Like the truck, the keychain was shaped like a taco.

"How much do you want for it?"

"Three hundred."

Luke sighed in frustration. "Will you take a check?"

"Absolutely."

~

Luke parallel-parked the taco in front of Carley's place and trudged around the back, where he knocked on her door and waited. A light came on, and after the sounds of shuffling, the door opened a crack. Carley peered out of the opening.

"Luke. What's happening?"

"Did you hear about Gridley?"

She nodded. "I did. I was trying to call you."

"My phone is probably at the bottom of the river."

For the first time, she seemed to notice Luke's disheveled appearance.

"What happened to you? Are you all right?!"

"You wouldn't believe what I've been through tonight. I interviewed a woman who was Ben Gerritt's *mistress*. Some pickup truck ran me off the road! I'm driving a damn *taco-*"

"Taco?" She seemed confused.

"I recorded the interview, but that went into the drink along with my phone."

"When did all of this happen?"

"In the last few hours. It's been a long night."

"Did you want to come in?"

"Normally, I'd like nothing more, but to be honest, I just want to get home, get into some dry clothes, and go to sleep. I just wanted to make sure you knew what was happening. If someone other than me contacts you, *be on guard.*"

Carley nodded. "Don't worry. I will be. Now, what's this about a taco?"

Luke gave her a half-hearted smile. "I'll tell you tomorrow."

~

Luke got to his apartment a short time later. The taco barely fit under his covered parking space. He trudged through the complex's courtyard, around the glowing swimming pool, to his apartment, where he noticed a sliver of light shining along the edge of his door. It was ajar.

Shit.

He approached warily, set one hand on the door, and shoved it open. It swung in with a creak.

His apartment was trashed. He looked around the living room. Drawers were ripped out and dumped on the floor. Shelves had been knocked over. Someone had given the place a thorough ransacking.

"Any of you assholes still here?" he called out to any intruders who might possibly still be inside.

There was no response. Just silence.

"Well okay then," Luke muttered and walked inside.

He stripped off his shirt and pants, dried himself with a towel the apartment ransackers had considerately left strewn on the floor, and collapsed on the couch, where he immediately fell asleep.

~

The sharp ring of a telephone rattled Luke awake. He looked around, groggy and confused, trying to get his bearings. His trashed surroundings got him up to speed.

He fumbled through the mess, searching for his landline, which he finally located under a pile of dirty laundry.

"Hello?" Luke grumbled.

"Luke, get to the civic center downtown," Carley ordered. "There's a press conference scheduled for 10:30. Ben Gerritt running for governor."

~

A large crowd was seated in the auditorium. For such a hastily announced public event, quite a few of the affiliate stations from Albuquerque had managed to make it to Farmington in time for the big show. All told, Luke counted camera crews from a half-dozen TV stations.

Ben Gerritt was standing at the lectern, wrapping up his announcement speech. That signature grin was plastered across his face. Luke and Carley were seated in the back of the audience.

"So I guess that's all I have to tell you at the moment. But if y'all have any questions, I'll certainly do my best to answer them for you. Then I'd better get my nose to the grindstone. I've been out of politics for quite a while now, and my advisors keep reminding me that this business of running for governor is a lot of work."

Luke could feel his lip curling.

Gerritt laughed, and as if on cue, the audience

chuckled along with him. Camera flashes went off, as a number of reporters jumped to their feet with questions. Gerritt nodded to a young reporter seated to the side of Luke and Carley.

"Mr. Gerritt, is it true that construction of the sports arena may not be completed by the original summer deadline?" she asked.

"Well, I'm not too tied into the actual construction, but I was just talking to Jake Dupuis this morning, and from the sounds of it, I'm afraid that may be true. He's looking at completing it by Christmas, I believe."

A few more reporters stood to ask questions, which Gerritt answered with a smile and a familiar quip, but he seemed to be deliberately looking past Luke before taking each new question.

"Excuse me, Mr. Mayor!" Luke quickly jumped to his feet. The cameraman from KOB Eyewitness News swung his camera around to get Luke in the shot. "Luke Murphy with *The Aztec Review*. I was just wondering what you could tell me about the *history* of the arena project. It seems you have a long-running personal connection with the ownership of the land on which it's being built. Would you care to shed any light on that for me?"

Gerritt's mouth drew tight.

"Like I said earlier, I think I've spoken about that project quite a bit over the years. After all, I'm pretty proud of it. I think it's going to be a great service to this community-"

Luke interrupted. "Do you have any comment on the fact that the land it's being built on was owned by your former son-in-law, Harvey Pouch, who was *murdered* just last week?"

The audience began to murmur.

Camera shutters snapped as Gerritt's eyes narrowed.

"Well, I was obviously very sorry to hear about Harvey, but-"

"That land was sold to him while you were mayor, wasn't it? Who owns that land now?"

Gerritt stammered. "Well, *I* do, a portion of it at any rate-"

Luke interrupted him again. "And what did you *pay* for that land?"

The audience lurched to its feet. Flashes were popping throughout the crowd as the volume in the room grew louder.

Carley whispered in Luke's ear. "What the hell are you doing?"

"Any idea who *killed* Harvey Pouch?!" Luke continued.

Gerritt was regaining control now, motioning with his hands for the crowd to calm down. "Sir, I'm afraid I can't help you there." He made eye contact with Luke, bearing his teeth in a mean half-grin.

"Perhaps you should ask your friend in the local police..."

One of Gerritt's advisors stepped in front of him and grabbed the microphone.

"Sir," Gerritt's man said to Luke. "You are out of line. I'm afraid Mr. Gerritt will take no more questions at this time."

Now the audience was roiling with questions and shouting after Gerritt as he and his entourage walked off the stage and down the steps to the auditorium floor. Gerritt's face was crimson with rage.

Carley shuffled out into the aisle with Luke.

"That was stupid, Luke," she muttered. "That was really stupid."

Reporters were still trying to ask Gerritt questions, but the former mayor was forcing his way through the crowd, his men following close behind. He was heading for Luke. Gerritt surged up to Luke and Carley as they were almost to the exit. He slammed a hand on Luke's shoulder and spun him around.

For a second, Luke thought the old guy was going to haul off and punch him, but as he leaned in closer, Luke realized that wasn't the old man's style. Intimidation was what he handed out. His men did the dirty work.

"Mike Murphy's boy. You're a real troublemaker, aren't you? Just like your old man." He pressed a finger into Luke's chest. "You just can't leave well enough alone, can you? Let me tell you something-" He voice dropped to a hiss now. "You might be too young to understand this, but believe me, you have no idea what you're dealing with, son."

Luke struggled to respond, but words and his very breath had seeped from his lungs. Gerritt stared at him for a beat, ensuring that his message had come through loud and clear. Then he pulled his hand away, and he and his men continued up the aisle and out the front doors.

Carley waited until she and Luke had exited the auditorium and were out on the sidewalk; then she let him have it.

"Are you out of your mind?! You think that was *cute* what you pulled in there?"

"I'm going to expose that guy. I'm going to uncover all his dirty little secrets and make sure everyone in this city knows about them too."

"What you're going to do, Luke, is get yourself *killed*. Have you forgotten about your friend Gridley? These people are not messing around. You need to take it easy and think this thing through."

"That's *exactly* why that guy has gotten away with this stuff for all these years!" Luke shouted as he marched across the street to his vehicle.

"This is *serious,* Luke."

"I know this is serious," He replied as he climbed into his taco, started the engine, and took off in a cloud of thick, black smoke.

He pointed his ridiculous car in the direction of the new highway, where he floored it, intending to squeal the tires, gun the engine, and partake in some serious high-speed, road-rage therapy. Unfortunately, the taco had other ideas, and rather than taking off like a bat out of hell, Luke just hoped he'd be able to drive *at all.*

The engine sputtered and he looked at the gas gauge. It was down to E.

"Shit," he muttered under his breath as he pulled into a gas station.

He climbed angrily out of his taco car and hunted around for the gas tank, which he finally found tucked under the corner of a large slice of fiberglass avocado. He gripped the avocado in both hands, turned it counterclockwise, and set it on the corner of the corn tortilla fender.

God dammit. Did this thing take diesel or unleaded?

After some trial and error, regular proved the way to go.

The tank filled, Luke returned the handle to the side of the pump, and climbed back into the car. The taco started up in another cloud of black smoke. Luke stomped on the gas and pulled out of the station. He had just cranked the wheel to the right and executed an impressive U-turn, when he saw something green skitter across the street into the intersection.

Dammit. The gas cap.

He pulled the taco to the curb and marched
into the intersection, as a woman in a bright orange
Chevette came roaring around the corner, heading
right for him! She slammed on the brakes and
Luke shut his eyes, waiting to meet his maker. Tires
squealed and the Chevette's horn blared.

"Asshole!" The woman shouted.

Luke opened his eyes and stared into her
glowering face, which, he noted, was redder even
than the Styrofoam tomatoes glued to the side of his
tacomobile. Luke shrugged his shoulders and headed
back to the curb as the woman stepped on the gas
and swerved around him. She stopped at the light,
reached out an arm, and gave him the finger.

Up until then, he was more than willing to laugh
it off. After all, the entire scenario was utterly insane.
But that last gesture was the final straw, sending
Luke from bemused embarrassment to abject *rage*. He
gripped the avocado gas cap, and was just about to
haul off and throw it at the back of the woman's car,
when he caught himself. He flipped the cap over in
his hands. He looked back at the row of gas pumps at
the filling station.

Moments later, Luke was back in the car,
barreling down the new highway. He was nearly to
the area of the canyon where he used to play as a kid,
long before the highway or any of this had been built.
He turned at the next road, twisting and turning his

way down the streets, til he was driving through his childhood neighborhood.

~

Luke walked down the crumbling driveway. The yard was overgrown. The house was set back in a field of tall grass. The temperature was dropping. He pulled his coat closed to block the wind, and hurried to the front door. It took him some time to find his old key, and when he did, it took some finessing to work it into the lock. The deadbolt turned stiffly, but it eventually sprang open.

Luke pushed the door with some difficulty. He looked around the dusty front room and closed the door behind him. It was deathly quiet as he made his way past the walls of old family photos. He hadn't been in his father's house since his old man had passed away ten months ago. From the look of the place, you wouldn't think anyone had been there in a decade. It felt like it had been even longer.

Luke opened a cabinet in the living room and pulled out a bottle of the old man's scotch. He took a glass from the top shelf, blew off the dust, and poured himself four fingers of whiskey. He threw back a slug and took the glass and bottle with him as he headed to his father's office at the back of the house.

The place was dark. The shades were drawn, letting

in just the dimmest glow of daylight. Geological charts and graphs were scattered along the walls. Luke looked at some of the photographs. Numerous snapshots showed his father standing with drilling crews in front of oil rigs, or posing alongside fields of pumpjacks. Luke leaned against his father's desk and took another sip of scotch. His eyes settled on the row of file cabinets against the far wall. He walked over and started going through the records, flipping through file after file. Drawer after drawer. He wasn't sure what he was looking for, but he suspected the answer was somewhere in this office.

If Mike Murphy, the troublemaker Ben Gerritt had referred to, had the goods on the old mayor, he would never have let them go. He'd have kept the evidence tucked away, waiting for the light of day to eventually expose the truth.

Luke continued searching, working his way back through the files, year by year, until he finally came across something interesting. It was tucked in the back of the bottom drawer of the farthest-most cabinet. He pulled a sealed manila folder out of the drawer and set it on the table. On the flap was written one word: *Pouch*

Luke sat in his father's chair and picked up the old man's letter opener. He slipped the metal blade under the edge of the envelope's flap and gently sliced it open. Inside, he found a stack of neatly folded, yellowed papers. Luke took another drink and spread out the pages. He wasn't a geologist, but he'd seen enough of these charts over the years to have a basic understanding of how to read them.

He could still picture the way his father used to point to the relevant areas on the charts, showing Luke just what to look for, and rubbing his thumb and index finger together with a mischievous smile when he found it.

Studying these charts now, Luke Murphy saw *exactly* what he was looking for. It would have made his old man smile.

9.

If he was going to do this, he had to have a way to document it. Losing the recording of Faye Burkhardt had reminded Luke of one of the most important lessons of journalism: If you get a scoop, be *sure* you have the goods to back up your claims -- a source on record, a piece of damning evidence, *something* to serve as undeniable proof that the bombshell you're dropping on the public *cannot* be ignored. The sexier the better. This time, he would do everything in his power to ensure the evidence didn't end up at the bottom of a literal or figurative river.

Before he left his father's house, he took all of the old man's charts and diagrams, everything showing the true value of the former Pouch property, and stuffed then inside an old *Monopoly* box in the rec room closet down in the basement. Whoever had ransacked Luke's apartment hadn't thought to check his father's place yet, but if that idea came to them, Luke wanted to be sure they wouldn't have as easy a time finding the paper trail as he had.

He just hoped they wouldn't burn the place down.

His next step was Margo's apartment. He needed that infernal video camera of hers.

Sweet-talking his randy neighbor into letting him borrow her video camera was just as easy as Luke had hoped (and feared). The promises he'd had to make in order to get it, those were a littler harder to swallow.

"Don't forget, Luke, I'm holding you to our little bargain," Margo said with a wink and a terrifying wiggle as he headed for the taco truck.

"I won't forget," Luke said with a wince.

~

This time, Luke was making the trek to the floor of the canyon on foot. Hopefully, traveling lighter under cover of night would make him harder to locate. He assumed Gerritt and his guys would be looking for him. There was no way he was going to let them run him off the road again. Even if his temporary vehicle was one of the more absurd contraptions he'd ever seen, he was growing attached to it. And God only knew what Nick's third-string replacement car might be. It was hard to imagine a mode of transportation more embarrassing than a taco-mobile, but he wasn't in the mood to push his luck further.

He ditched the taco by a radio tower on the edge of Chokecherry Canyon, and carefully made his way down the sandstone cliffs. He used to climb into these channels and slot canyons as a kid. He knew them by heart. They were steep, and they were unstable in portions, but owing to the soft nature of sandstone, rain and weather tended to carve channels and slides into the sides, resulting in nature's version of steps and half-pipes, all of which made descending a fairly steep cliff a relatively easy affair.

The full moon helped him see where he was going, but Luke was all too aware of the fact that it also made it easier for Gerritt's men to see *him* as well, assuming they were monitoring the right places.

Fortunately, the trip to the canyon floor went faster than he had expected. The temperature was also dropping faster, however. It was a good thing he'd dressed fairly warmly for this. He fully expected to be out here for a while, staying as still as possible, waiting for something, *whatever it was,* to happen.

He raced across the canyon floor, heading in the direction of the sports arena. Once he got down the hillsides and away from the loose, sandy areas, the ground became firmer under foot – like the air-dried former riverbed that it was – and he was able to jog fairly comfortably for a couple of miles, until he was within range of the complex, but well away from the lights. That's where he set up shop, placing the camera on the tiny tripod Margo had lent him. He didn't turn the camera on. Not yet. But he was ready and waiting for the trucks to arrive.

Luke was growing drowsy by the time the action commenced. The cold ground was sapping the energy from his body, making him increasingly groggy. He was just starting to nod off when he heard the first rumble of a diesel engine. No sooner did he look up, than the first tanker truck roared past him, sending sand and dust billowing up into the air, just as it had the other night.

Luke switched on the camera and recorded the caravan as several more trucks rumbled by. Once the caravan had passed him by, Luke scooped up the camera, which was still recording, and took off running along the side of the dirt road. His arms and legs were pumping at a full sprint.

He could see the trucks well ahead of him now. They slowed as they neared the fenced perimeter of the arena complex, then grumbled through the fence and headed into the side of the main building. This was the same routine as the previous night.

Luke stopped to record them entering the building. He zoomed the camera in as close as possible as one by one the trucks disappeared into the giant structure.

He peered through the viewfinder, checking the shot. As soon as they had pulled inside, the massive door rumbled shut behind them. Luke stopped the camera and took off running again.

He was sweating and out of breath by the time he reached the arena grounds. He held back, getting a feel for what he would be dealing with. He'd been expecting massive security to be in place, but other than banks of floodlights and the fences that encircled the property, the yard seemed abandoned. There was no one in sight. No guards. No checkpoint. For the briefest moment, the lack of security made Luke doubt himself. Maybe this really was *just* a construction sight. Aside from chain-link fences and plenty of lights, why would they *need* to have armed guards around the place? What could someone do, *steal* the arena? The biggest concern just might be kids sneaking out and spray-painting their girlfriends' names on the sides of the buildings.

Then he recalled his father's paperwork.

And he remembered Gridley.

No, something was rotten. And this place was ground zero.

There wasn't a doubt in his mind.

Luke hit record on the camera and panned around the property, getting a good shot of the banner: "Gerritt Arena: Making Farmington Great Again!"

He zoomed in on every sign for Dupuis

Construction. Sweeping the camera around the property and following the fence line as it traveled up and down over the surrounding lot. He noticed a place where the fence climbed over a sandstone ridge, and the distance between the ground and the barbed wire top was much closer. In most areas, the fences looked to be around 16 feet high, but in that area it was probably just under nine. Luke pulled off his thick jacket, flung the camera strap around his shoulder, and headed for the ridge.

If he was going to take a chance on this, he might as well do it in the spot that offered him the lowest chance of falling on his ass. He wrapped his coat around his waist, ran to the fence, and started to climb. Aside from the jangle of the wire mesh, everything was quiet. No one came running out to scream at him. He stopped at the top, working the fingers of his left hand through the fence, and carefully pulling the coat from around his waist. He gauged the distance from the top of the chain-link to the strands of barbed wire, pulled his arm back, and swung the coat towards the glimmering tines. His first attempt fell short, but his second go was a success. The coat flew up over the wire. One arm fell over the side, while the other stayed gripped in his hand. Luke pulled down with all the strength he could muster, and tied the arms together *tight.* In the process, he managed to pull the barbed wire down more than a foot, and wrapped it in the thick fabric of his coat.

Climbing over was surprisingly easy. His pant leg snagged on one of the metal tines as he swung his leg over - he heard the denim tear as he pulled it free – but he was otherwise unscathed when he landed in the dirt on the other side.

Once inside the fenced complex, he ran to the corner of the nearest building and switched the camera back on, again sweeping it around and recording anything he saw that would clearly identify where he was. Then he pulled back into the shadows, weighing his next move. He was breathing heavily now. All those years behind the news desk, driving from one story to the next, were catching up on him.

Assuming he survived this little escapade, he had to start exercising!

His breath billowed in the cold winter air as he looked around wildly. He needed to find a way to get inside the complex's largest building.

Light glimmered over the edges of a thick metal cable that ran from the ground up to a heavy canvas awning covering the windows along one side of the half-completed arena.

More cables ran around the side of the structure at 20-foot intervals. Luke homed in on one cable in particular, which sat back in the shadows. He slung the video camera over his shoulder and ran over to it. He ran his fingers over the braided metal. It was thick and almost sticky, covered in some sort of tacky coating. The surface was free of any metal slivers or sharp edges. He wiped his hands on his shirt to rub off the perspiration, then he grabbed ahold of the cable, and started to shimmy his way up.

Thanks to the coating on the wire, it was surprisingly easy to maintain a grip on the cable as he inched his way upward, foot by foot. He made a conscious decision not to look down, however, knowing that if he did, he would panic at how high he was climbing. If he fell, it would almost certainly be fatal. There was no choice now. No looking back. He just had to go for it.

His muscles were screaming by the time he reached the top. With his last bit of strength, he swung himself up onto the ledge that surrounded the highest level of the arena, and stopped to knead his arms and legs, coaxing blood to the burning tissues. When he finally got to his feet, he discovered that the openings to the interior of the building were all covered with sheets of plywood.

Shit.

Luke felt along the edges of the nearest panel. His fingers were painfully sore from the climb. He looked around for a pry-bar, a piece of rebar, *anything* he could use to force his away inside, but the areas around him were bare. It appeared he had nowhere else to go. There was also no way in *hell* he was going back down that cable; he'd lose his grip before he'd made it halfway back to the ground.

He'd just have to keep looking.

Luke made his way around the outer ledge, stopping at each boarded-up section, examining it for weaknesses. Finally, he found one area that wasn't perfectly aligned. He leaned on it with his hands, and it budged, shifting inward just slightly. He set the camera down away from the edge, and pressed his shoulder against the wood, shoving harder and harder against the plywood barrier, until little by little, it began to move. Finally, with every bit of strength he could muster, he rammed it one last time, and it fell inward, with Luke tumbling in behind.

He grunted in pain as he fell over the debris and landed on the concrete bleachers inside. He got to his feet, but it took a moment for his mind to reconcile the scope and startling contradictions of what he was seeing. He was far up in the shadows of a massive arena. There were thousands upon thousands of seats, but only the lower areas were illuminated.

One thing was certain though, for such an unlikely cover, Gerritt and Jake Dupuis were definitely being thorough. They really were building an arena. Whether it would ever be *used,* that was another matter.

It was then, as Luke's eyes began to adjust to

155

the light and he looked past the seats, across the distance, to the building's ground level, that the mind-boggling truth of the situation sank in. His jaw dropped as he saw what was really happening in this building.

His father had been right.

Gerritt and his boys had cracked it.

The floor of the arena was *covered* in a maze of metal pipes and valves, a sprawling network of production trees. There were no pumpjacks in this operation, there was no need for them. This place was producing, and it was pumping out dividends.

Oil.

The former Pouch property was sitting on a gold mine, one that had almost been tapped decades ago, but whoever had owned the place back then had stopped exploring, or lost control of the land, before they'd drilled down to the *true* wealth beneath their feet. But somehow, Gerritt had known what was down there, and he'd done everything in his power to make sure he had first dibs, even if it meant having his less than beloved son-in-law sit on the nest while he waited for his plans to hatch. Finally, long after his time as mayor was done, after he'd used a few remarkably ballsy maneuvers to get that property under his control, Ben Gerritt, with the help of Jake Dupuis, was pumping that oil out of the ground *right under the noses* of the people of Farmington. And

Gerritt had the nerve to call the arena the city's best shot at an economic recovery, while he was helping himself to one of the biggest oil reservoirs in the state's history, on land that, by any just measure, should have rightly belonged to the city!

Luke reached through the window and retrieved the video camera. The tanker trucks were lined up at the far edge of the floor, where a crew of workers was hooking them up to the Christmas tree of supply valves. Luke pressed record and zoomed in on the trucks.

Down at ground level, the crew, all of them clad in hardhats and work gear, was working furiously. The noise of the machinery muffled their shouted exchanges as they switched the connections on a caravan of trucks. Luke got a clear shot of one of the workers as he disconnected a hose from a tanker. Another crew member gave him the order to pull forward, and motioned for one of the new arrivals to pull up. Once the new tanker was in place, the cable was secured, and the guy in charge gave the all clear to start the flow again.

He couldn't imagine how long they must have been cycling the tankers in and out of this place. Months? *Years?*

The Gerritt Arena wouldn't be opening anytime soon!

Luke crouched in the shadows and tried to move into position to get a better shot of the trucks. He had to get as much footage of all this as he could.

One of the drivers of the newly arrived tankers leaned against the side of his truck, wiping sweat from his brow as he waited for his turn to pull forward. He sighed and looked up into the dark shadows of the surrounding arena. Then he saw a short flash of red. The man leaned forward, squinting into the darkness until he saw it again. He turned and walked over to a man standing in the shadows nearby. The other man stepped forward, the light hitting his dark eyes and thick black moustache. The driver shouted something into the moustache man's ear as he pointed in Luke's direction.

That was all Luke needed to see.

Time to bail.

He looked around the arena. There was no way he could make it down to the floor without them getting there before him. He shut off the camera and climbed back onto the ledge, where he peeked down over the edge.

The world began to spin.

Hell no.

He turned to the cable, shaking his head.

He'd never make it.

There had to be an easier way.

He climbed back in through the opening and ran around the top of the arena til he came to a stairway. He rushed down, emerging in a large, dark corridor. A string of work lights hung from the ceiling, running down the length of the hall. They provided minimal illumination. Luke headed to the right, doing his best to stay in the shadows. He was partway down the hallway when a familiar voice called out behind him.

"Hold it right there!" the voice shouted.

Luke recognized him immediately.

Sonny West.

"I said stop, Luke!"

Shit. He'd recognized him.

Luke dropped the camera, letting it hang free around his neck as he put his hands up in surrender. He turned around and saw Sonny's silhouette slowly moving toward him through the darkness. He was walking down the center of the corridor, popping in and out of view as he passed through each pool of light from overhead. Finally, he stepped out into the light, giving Luke a nice, clear view of the gun Sonny had trained on him.

"Whatever you've got there, put it on the floor *now!*"

Luke slowly lifted the strap from around his neck and set the camera on the floor, aiming it down the hall at Sonny and pushing the record button. He dropped the strap over the front of the viewfinder, covering the flashing red light.

Sonny moved closer, the disappointed look on his face growing more apparent with each step.

"Murphy, how many times did I tell you to mind your own business? Why did you have to keep poking around?"

"Sonny, what in the hell are you doing mixed up in all this?"

"I think you can guess."

"So, you're in on this with them?"

"Wake up Luke, everyone in the system is in on this. We don't have that much choice about it."

Sonny was still walking toward him.

"You're robbing this town blind," Luke said.

"It's not the city's property."

Luke shrugged. "Maybe so, but it sure as hell wasn't sold for what it's worth." He nodded toward the interior of the arena. The rumble of the equipment echoed around them. "Especially when you factor in what's going on out there."

Sonny continued his slow advance.

"Whose behind this whole thing?" Luke asked.

"I think you've already guessed that."

"Gerritt...Dupuis?"

"Bingo."

"How long has this been going on?"

"What does that matter?" Sonny asked.

"They can't use this arena cover forever. Sooner or later people are going to demand to know what the holdup is. Gerritt's covered the bulk of this project, but the city's given him tax breaks. They've covered some of the expense. They're paying to extend the highway out here! How long before someone else gets in here and discovers Gerritt has built this thing on one of the biggest oil reservoirs in state history, and he's illegally pumping it dry before he ever plans to open this place to the public?"

"How do you know it's one of the biggest in history?"

"My father was the city's geologist when Gerritt started maneuvering to get his hands on this place 30 years ago. He knew it was a gold mine. Gerritt and his guys must have scared him pretty good to keep him from talking."

Sonny was getting closer. He was still holding the gun, but his hand was wavering slightly.

"Are you gonna kill me?" Luke asked. "Like you killed Gridley?"

"I didn't kill Detective Gridley!"

"Of course you did," Luke spat.

"Gerritt's guys killed Gridley! OK, Luke?"

"So what are *you* gonna do, man?" Luke challenged.

Sonny reached behind him, pulling out a set of handcuffs.

"Look, I don't want to have to do this," Sonny muttered. "Dammit, Luke, why couldn't you have minded your own business just once?"

Luke just stared him in the eyes.

161

"Turn around, Luke!"

Luke turned around, still holding up his arms.

"Get down on your knees and put your hands behind your back."

"Just tell me this, why in the hell is Gerritt choosing to run for Governor *now?*"

Luke glanced down at the camera near his feet. His eyes locked on the strap.

"Get down on your knees *now,* Luke!"

Luke dropped to one knee.

"It just doesn't make sense to me. He's finally got this system working for him. Why the distraction of running for office again after all this time?"

Sonny seemed annoyed. "Probably exactly that, a distraction. The excuses for this place not getting completed are getting harder and harder to pass off. Now he's running for *governor,* because he loves his city and this *state* so much. That should use up a lot of ink while he campaigns..."

Sonny was starting to relax. Luke could hear it in his voice.

"Probably a good way to avoid prosecution too, right?" Luke pressed. "If he's governor, he'll make sure no one is poking around here. Hold 'em off for four years. Maybe eight. Keep apologizing for working so hard for the good of New Mexico, while Dupuis works back here, getting every last drop out of the ground before they cap it off and finish this building. Or hell, maybe they'll never finish the building. Just cap it. Cover it, and walk away."

"Look, man," Sonny said. "Just shut the hell up and let me get these cuffs on you. This shit is above my pay grade."

"Yeah, I suppose you're right," Luke agreed.

"Gimme your hands, Luke," Sonny said as he lowered his weapon.

Luke eyed the camera strap again.

"Hey Sonny, any interest in letting me join that softball team still?"

"You've gotta be kidding, man…"

"You sure?" Luke muttered. "Cause I've still got a good swing."

God only knew what he'd have to do to make this up to Margo.

Suddenly, Luke grabbed the strap and spun around, swinging the camera through the air and smashing it into Sonny's face. The gun and handcuffs flew from Sonny's hands as he recoiled in pain.

Luke leapt to his feet, punching Sonny square in the face as hard as he could. A struggle ensued as the two men fought and tumbled across the cement floor. Sonny scrambled for the gun, but Luke came down on his back with two balled up fists, knocking the breath out of him. Sonny rolled over and blindly kicked Luke in the face.

Finally, after several close calls, Luke managed to

knock the gun down a drainage opening in the floor along the side of the corridor. It clattered out of sight. Sonny came at him again, but Luke just managed to grab the camera by its strap and smash Sonny in the face with it again. This time, it hit home, knocking the crooked cop out cold.

Luke looked at the camera.

Jesus. Hopefully the recording was still OK.

He looked at the side of the camera. It was completely smashed in. He held the housing in his hands and managed to force the storage slot open. The memory card appeared to be intact. He pulled it out and slipped it into his pocket, then he threw down the camera and took off running down the hall.

He managed to make it down several tunnels and stairways without being seen. Then he found himself in what looked to be a large loading dock. No one was around, and except for several pools of light in the middle of the empty concrete floor, the space was dark. He could hear men shouting and running through the corridors overhead, but for now, he was alone.

Luke ran over to a large work truck at one end of the room. Spools of heavy cable sat on the vehicle's flatbed. He leaned in through the driver's side window. The keys were in the ignition! He climbed back down and jogged over to the massive doors. He couldn't find any sort of control. There was no visible way to open them. Finding nothing he could use to force it, Luke climbed up into the cab of the truck, closed the door behind him, and started it up. He revved the engine a few times, and rolled up the windows as the area quickly filled with thick smoke. Anyone who was looking for him would know *exactly* where to find him now.

Luke pulled the seatbelt across his chest, slipped the transmission into gear, and stomped on the accelerator. The truck leapt forward, tires squealing, engine roaring as Luke worked his way up through the gears. He'd need to have as much momentum as possible. The engine was screaming as the truck roared down the length of the garage. Then, with Luke at the helm, it smashed into the door, blasting it apart in a cloud of splintering metal ribbons, and knocking it from its tracks.

The truck barreled out of the arena in a cacophony of screaming, tearing, twisting metal. Luke shifted gears and sped up, charging through the work site and dodging workers and vehicles as they tried to block his way. He glanced nervously at his side mirrors. Sweat was dripping down his face as he pulled the memory card out of his pocket, kissed it, and let out a nervous, adrenaline-fueled yell.

He had to get into town before any of Gerritt's guys could catch up to him. He knew right where he was headed, and though he wanted to break the story himself, in print, there was no time for that, not at the moment. He had to get to the KOB station and get this on the air.

He checked his side mirrors again for headlights. Nothing yet.

This was going to be tight, but he just might make it...

10.

Luke sat at the bar watching the TV. The video he had shot inside the arena was playing for the umpteenth time. He was a print guy, so seeing this footage, *his footage,* playing on a station he had always viewed as the competition, filled him with mixed feelings. Of course, he still had *plenty* to write about. There would be lots of time to revel in the story he had broken, one that was proving to have long legs in the national news cycle. But for now, all he wanted was a drink.

The bar at the Skyliner was empty. Not too many people came in for drinks before 11 in the morning, but Luke needed it. Rene came over with a white Russian, which he set it front of Luke, who looked down at the mixed cocktail.

None of those layers Ben Gerritt professed to enjoy.

Nothing going on below the surface.

Luke gave the swizzle stick an extra swirl, just to be safe, and set it on the napkin. He took a sip of his drink as the KOB Eyewitness News reporter recapped the morning's top story while the video feed cut to close-ups of the elaborate system of supply valves on the arena floor.

"Citizens are still in shock this morning at the news that Jacob Dupuis and gubernatorial candidate Ben Gerritt were behind one of the most bizarre and far-reaching scams in recent memory. While much of the City of Farmington's new sports complex is nearly completed, the biggest attraction, the huge stadium arena, had long been plagued by unexplained delays. One look at this footage taken by area reporter Luke Murphy tells us why."

He heard a pair of heels clinking on the tile floor behind him.

"I can't believe you gave the biggest story of the year to our competition," Carley said. "And it wasn't even a newspaper!"

Luke turned and looked at her. "I had to made a judgment call. I figured getting the story out there as soon as possible was my best chance at not getting killed. Can I get you a drink?"

"Little early for me still," she said as she took a seat beside him and picked up his water glass.

"Shouldn't we be covering this?" Luke asked.

Carley shrugged. "We already lost the news cycle, might as well relax. Besides, nobody reads our paper anyway."

"Maybe they will now? I have a feeling we're just

scratching the surface."

She laughed. "You may have something there."

They turned back to the TV, where a crowd of onlookers and camera men was lined up by the curb in front of the police headquarters. Two police cars, their lights flashing, but their sirens silenced, led a caravan of cars. They pulled past the main entrance, allowing the white Suburban behind them to stop at the end of the front walkway in front of the police station. Two police officers climbed out of the vehicle, leading Ben Gerritt between them. Save for the unusual surroundings, Gerritt looked much the same as always under his signature hat, but his trademark grin, his knowing smirk, that was missing now.

"Why don't they have him cuffed?" Luke observed.

"He's Ben Gerritt, former mayor and local hero. They're probably giving him what they can of his dignity."

"Seems like a mistake to me," Luke said as he took a sip of his drink.

The reporter's voice chimed in again.

"Gerritt is being brought in for questioning now. Lot of people here looking for answers today."

The crowd moved in as Gerritt headed up the walk towards the building. The officers pushed back against the surging crowd as Gerritt followed another officer to the top of the stairs.

"The folks all used to love him. Maybe they still

do," Carley observed as she reached for his water.

Luke was quiet. He was watching the scene on screen intently.

There was a sinking feeling in the pit of his stomach.

Luke lowered his drink as he watched Gerritt's eyes move from the crowd to the handle of the nearest officer's weapon. The safety holster was unbuckled.

"Shit." Luke muttered.

Before anyone realized what was happening, Gerritt reached over, pulled the gun from the officer's holster, and set it under his chin.

Someone screamed.

Ben Gerritt paused for a split second, then he pulled the trigger.

The broadcast cut back to the stunned anchors in the studio.

Carley choked on her water.

Rene, who was wiping down the bar, froze in place, blinking.

"On second thought," Carley said. "I think I'll have that drink after all."

***

Once the shock of the day's events had worn off, and the effects of their drinks had begun to dissipate, Carley came to the topic they had been dancing around for days.

"So let me ask you something, Luke. Are we gonna give this a go or what?"

"What do you mean *this?*"

"You and me. *Us.* Are you planning on sticking around here for a while, or are you gonna bail on Farmington again?"

"I'm planning on sticking around."

"Well, then what's the deal? Why does it feel like you're keeping your distance?"

"What are you talking about?" Luke exclaimed. "I didn't know what your situation was. I was giving you your space."

"I never asked for it."

"OK. Then what do you want from me?"

"Well first of all, I think you need to make up for giving the scoop on the arena story to another outlet."

"And what do you have in mind exactly?" Luke asked as he leaned in closer.

"I have a few ideas," She said. "Maybe we could head over to your place and talk them over."

"Oh," Luke said, suddenly remembering Margo and her camera. "I have a feeling my neighbor might think she has first dibs."

Carley put her hand on his shoulder and pushed him back. "Why would she think that?"

"I borrowed her camera and sort of smashed Sonny's

face with it."

"Is that it?" She dropped a wad of money on the counter to cover their drinks.

"That's it," he said as they stood and headed for the door.

"Well tell her tough shit, 'cause I've got first position on this debt, and you better believe I'm collecting."

Get the very first
BRICK RANSOM
story for
FREE

Building a relationship with my readers is one of the most exciting parts of my writing career. I occasionally send newsletters with information on upcoming releases, special offers, and other exclusive content, like the free BRICK RANSOM story I'm offering now.

To get the story and see how it all began, please sign up at www.mikeattebery.com

Did you enjoy this book?

You can make a huge difference.

Reviews are the most powerful tools in my utility belt when it comes to getting attention for my writing. As an indie author, resources for advertising and media exposure are limited, fortunately, word of mouth is every bit as effective.

The support of readers means the world to me.

Honest reviews of my books are invaluable in bringing them to the attention of other readers. Word of mouth is my greatest weapon!

If you enjoyed this book, I would be extremely grateful if you could take a moment and leave a review.

Thank you very much for your support.

Acknowledgments

Thanks as always to Jason Croatto for the excellent cover art and interior layout!

Thank you to Liz Attebery for her thorough proofreading.

Thanks to my readers for their support of my writing over all these years.

And of course, thank you most of all to Stephanie and Charley. I couldn't do *any* of this without your support.

About the Author

Mike Attebery grew up in Farmington, New Mexico and Madison, Connecticut. He is the author of the Brick Ransom thrillers *Billionaires, Bullets, Exploding Monkeys*; *Seattle On Ice*; and *Bloody Pulp*. His other books include *On/Off* and *Rosé in Saint Tropez*. He lives in Seattle, Washington with his wife and daughter. Mike is currently at work on a new four-book series.

Made in the USA
Las Vegas, NV
13 October 2021